Praise for *Krik? Krak!*

FINALIST FOR THE NATIONAL BOOK AWARD

"Steeped in the myths and lore that sustained generations of Haitians, *Krik? Krak!* demonstrates the healing power of storytelling." —*San Francisco Chronicle*

"Virtually flawless . . . If the news from Haiti is too painful to read, read this book instead and understand the place more deeply than you ever thought possible."
—*Washington Post Book World*

"The voices of *Krik? Krak!* . . . encapsulate whole lifetimes of experience. Harsh, passionate, lyrical."—*The Seattle Times*

"Steady-handed yet devastating . . . In Haiti, where politics are lethal and women are condemned to suffering and death by men who envy and fear their powers, hope does indeed seem ludicrous, but in Danticat's fiction, mind and spirit soar above the pain and horrors of life." —*Booklist*

"Danticat beautifully balances the poverty, despair, and brutality her characters endure with magic and myth. For many characters, she also explores the inevitable clash between traditions of Haitian home life and a new American culture. Principally mothers and daughters confront each other in these cultural and intergenerational wars, wars that would be emotionally devastating were it not for the indomitable presence of love . . . Highly recommended."—*Library Journal*

Krik? Krak!

Also by Edwidge Danticat

FICTION
Claire of the Sea Light
The Dew Breaker
The Farming of Bones
Breath, Eyes, Memory

NONFICTION
Create Dangerously: The Immigrant Artist at Work
Brother, I'm Dying
After the Dance: A Walk Through Carnival in Jacmel

FOR YOUNG READERS
Anacaona, Golden Flower
Behind the Mountains
Eight Days
The Last Mapou

AS EDITOR
The Butterfly's Way: Voices From the Haitian Dyaspora in the United States

The Beacon Best of 2000: Great Writing by Women and Men of All Colors and Cultures

The Best American Essays 2011

Haiti Noir

Krik? Krak!

edwidge danticat

The following stories have been previously published, some of them in a slightly different form: "Children of the Sea" appeared under the title "From the Ocean Floor" in *Short Fiction by Women* (October 1993); "A Wall of Fire Rising" appeared under the title "A Wall of Fire" in *Cymbals: The National Student Literary Magazine* (Summer 1991); "The Missing Peace" in *Just a Moment* (Pine Grove Press, Fall 1992) and in *The Caribbean Writer* (July 1994); "Between the Pool and the Gardenias" in *The Caribbean Writer* (Summer 1993) and in *Best of the Small Presses* (Pushcart Press 1994) (winner of the Pushcart Prize) and also in *Monologues By Women* (Heinemann 1994) and "Night Women" appeared under the title "Voices in a Dream" in *The Caribbean Writer* (Summer 1993) as well as in Brown University's *Clerestory* (July 1994).

All rights reserved.
Published by
Soho Press Inc.
853 Broadway
New York, NY 10003

Library of Congress Cataloging-in-Publication Data

Danticat, Edwidge,
[Short stories. Selections]
Krik? krak! / Edwidge Danticat.

ISBN 978-1-61695-700-1
eISBN 978-1-56947-802-8

I. Title.
PS3554.A5815A6 2015
813'.54—dc23   2015034104

Printed in the United States of America

10 9 8 7 6 5

Krik? Krak! Somewhere by the seacoast I feel a breath
of warm sea air and hear the laughter of children.
An old granny smokes her pipe,
surrounded by the village children . . .
"We tell the stories so that the young ones
will know what came before them.
They ask Krik? we say Krak!
Our stories are kept in our hearts."

— SAL SCALORA,
"White Darkness/Black Dreamings"
Haiti: Feeding The Spirit

Krik? Krak!

contents

· ❁ ❁ ❁ ·

Children of the Sea

· ❀ ❀ ❀ ·

They say behind the mountains are more mountains. Now I know it's true. I also know there are timeless waters, endless seas, and lots of people in this world whose names don't matter to anyone but themselves. I look up at the sky and I see you there. I see you crying like a crushed snail, the way you cried when I helped you pull out your first loose tooth. Yes, I did love you then. Somehow when I looked at you, I thought of fiery red ants. I wanted you to dig your fingernails into my skin and drain out all my blood.

I don't know how long we'll be at sea. There are thirty-six other deserting souls on this little boat with me. White sheets with bright red spots float as our sail.

When I got on board I thought I could still smell the semen and the innocence lost to those sheets. I look up there and I think of you and all those times you resisted. Sometimes I felt like you wanted to, but I knew you wanted me to respect you. You thought I was testing your will, but all I wanted was to be near you. Maybe it's like you've always said. I imagine too much. I am afraid I am going to start having nightmares once we get deep at sea. I really hate having the sun in my face all day long. If you see me again, I'll be so dark.

Your father will probably marry you off now, since I am gone. Whatever you do, please don't marry a soldier. They're almost not human.

· ❋ ·

haiti est comme tu l'as laissé. yes, just the way you left it. bullets day and night. same hole. same everything. i'm tired of the whole mess. i get so cross and irritable. i pass the time by chasing roaches around the house. i pound my heel on their heads. they make me so mad. everything makes me mad. i am cramped inside all day. they've closed the schools since the army took over. no one is mentioning the old president's name. papa burnt all his campaign posters and old buttons. manman buried her buttons in a hole behind the house. she thinks he might come back. she says she will unearth them when he does. no one comes out of their house. not a single person. papa wants me to throw out those tapes of your radio shows. i destroyed some music tapes, but i still have your voice. i thank god you got out when you did. all the other youth federation members have disappeared. no one has heard from them. i think they might all be in prison. maybe they're all dead. papa worries a little about you. he doesn't hate you as much as you think. the other day i heard him asking manman, do you think the boy is dead? manman said she didn't know. i think he regrets being so mean to you. i don't sketch my butterflies anymore because i don't even like seeing the sun. besides, manman says that butterflies can bring news. the bright ones bring happy news and the black ones warn us of deaths. we have our whole lives ahead of us. you used to say that, remember? but then again things were so very different then.

· ❧ ·

There is a pregnant girl on board. She looks like she might be our age. Nineteen or twenty. Her face is covered with scars that look like razor marks. She is short and speaks in a singsong that reminds me of the villagers in the north. Most of the other people on the boat are much older than I am. I have heard that a lot of these boats have young children on board. I am glad this one does not. I think it would break my heart watching some little boy or girl every single day on this sea, looking into their empty faces to remind me of the hopelessness of the future in our country. It's hard enough with the adults. It's hard enough with me.

I used to read a lot about America before I had to study so much for the university exams. I am trying to think, to see if I read anything more about Miami. It is sunny. It doesn't snow there like it does in other parts of America. I can't tell exactly how far we are from there. We might be barely out of our own shores. There are no borderlines on the sea. The whole thing looks like one. I cannot even tell if we are about to drop off the face of the earth. Maybe the world is flat and we are going to find out, like the navigators of old. As you know, I am not very religious. Still I pray every night that we won't hit a storm. When I do manage to sleep, I dream that we are caught in one hurricane after another. I dream that the winds come of the sky and claim us for the sea. We go under and no one hears from us again.

I am more comfortable now with the idea of dying. Not that I have completely accepted it, but I know that it might happen. Don't be mistaken. I really do not want to be a martyr. I know I am no good to anybody dead, but if that is what's coming, I know I cannot just scream at it and tell it to go away.

I hope another group of young people can do the radio show. For a long time that radio show was my whole life. It was nice to have radio like that for a while, where we could talk about what we wanted from government, what we wanted for the future of our country.

There are a lot of Protestants on this boat. A lot of them see themselves as Job or the Children of Israel. I think some of them are hoping something will plunge down from the sky and part the sea for us. They say the Lord gives and the Lord takes away. I have never been given very much. What was there to take away?

· ❧ ·

if only i could kill. if i knew some good *wanga* magic, i would wipe them off the face of the earth. a group of students got shot in front of fort dimanche prison today. they were demonstrating for the bodies of the radio six. that is what they are calling you all. the radio six. you have a name. you have a reputation. a lot of people think you are dead like the others. they want the bodies turned over to the families. this afternoon, the army finally did give some bodies back. they told the families to go collect them at the rooms for indigents at the morgue. our neighbor madan roger came home with her son's head and not much else. honest to god, it was just his head. at the morgue, they say a car ran over him and took the head off his body. when madan roger went to the morgue, they gave her the head. by the time we saw her, she had been carrying the head all over port-au-prince. just to show what's been done to her son. the macoutes by the house were laughing at her. they asked her if that was her dinner. it took ten people to hold her back from jumping on them. they would have killed her, the dogs. i will never go outside again. not even in the yard to breathe the air. they are always watching you, like vultures. at night i can't sleep. i count the bullets in the dark. i keep wondering if it is true. did you really get out? i wish there was some way i could be sure that you really went away. yes, i will. i will keep writing like we promised to do. i hate it, but i will keep writing. you keep writing too, okay? and when we see each other again, it will seem like we lost no time.

· ❧ ·

Today was our first real day at sea. Everyone was vomiting with each small rocking of the boat. The faces around me are showing their first charcoal layer of sunburn. "Now we will never be mistaken for Cubans," one man said. Even though some of the Cubans are black too. The man said he was once on a boat with a group of Cubans. His boat had stopped to pick up the Cubans on an island off the Bahamas. When the Coast Guard came for them, they took the Cubans to Miami and sent him back to Haiti. Now he was back on the boat with some papers and documents to show that the police in Haiti were after him. He had a broken leg too, in case there was any doubt.

One old lady fainted from sunstroke. I helped revive her by rubbing some of the salt water on her lips. During the day it can be so hot. At night, it is so cold. Since there are no mirrors, we look at each others faces to see just how frail and sick we are starting to look.

Some of the women sing and tell stories to each other to appease the vomiting. Still, I watch the sea. At night, the sky and the sea are one. The stars look so huge and so close. They make for very bright reflections in the sea. At times I feel like I can just reach out and pull a star down from the sky as though it is a breadfruit or a calabash or something that could be of use to us on this journey.

When we sing, *Beloved Haiti, there is no place like you. I had to leave you before I could understand you,* some of the women start crying. At times, I just want to stop in the middle of the song and cry myself. To hide my tears, I pretend like I am getting another attack of nausea, from the sea smell. I no longer join in the singing.

You probably do not know much about this, because you have always been so closely watched by your father in that well-guarded house with your genteel mother. No, I am not making fun of you for this. If anything, I am jealous. If I was a girl, maybe I would have been at home and not out politicking and getting myself into something like this. Once you have been at sea for a couple of days, it smells like every fish you have ever eaten, every crab you have ever caught, every jellyfish that has ever bitten your leg. I am so tired of the smell. I am also tired of the way the people on this boat are starting to stink. The pregnant girl, Célianne, I don't know how she takes it. She stares into space all the time and rubs her stomach.

I have never seen her eat. Sometimes the other women offer her a piece of bread and she takes it, but she has no food of her own. I cannot help feeling like she will have this child as soon as she gets hungry enough.

She woke up screaming the other night. I thought she had a stomachache. Some water started coming into the boat in the spot where she was sleeping. There is a crack at the bottom of the boat that looks as though, if it gets any bigger, it will split the boat in two. The captain cleared us aside and used some tar to clog up the hole. Everyone started asking him if it was okay, if they were going to be okay. He said he hoped the Coast Guard would find us soon.

You can't really go to sleep after that. So we all stared at the tar by the moonlight. We did this until dawn. I cannot help but wonder how long this tar will hold out.

· ❊ ·

papa found your tapes. he started yelling at me, asking if I was crazy keeping them. he is just waiting for the gasoline ban to be lifted so we can get out of the city. he is always pestering me these days because he cannot go out driving his van. all the american factories are closed. he kept yelling at me about the tapes. he called me selfish, and he asked if i hadn't seen or heard what was happening to man-crazy whores like me. i shouted that i wasn't a whore. he had no business calling me that. he pushed me against the wall for disrespecting him. he spat in my face. i wish those macoutes would kill him. i wish he would catch a bullet so we could see how scared he really is. he said to me, i didn't send your stupid trouble maker away. i started yelling at him. yes, you did. yes, you did. yes, you did, you pig peasant. i don't know why i said that. he slapped me and kept slapping me really hard until manman came and grabbed me away from him. i wish one of those bullets would hit me.

· ❧ ·

The tar is holding up so far. Two days and no more leaks. Yes, I am finally an African. I am even darker than your father. I wanted to buy a straw hat from one of the ladies, but she would not sell it to me for the last two gourdes I have left in change. Do you think your money is worth anything to me here? she asked me. Sometimes, I forget where I am. If I keep daydreaming like I have been doing, I will walk off the boat to go for a stroll. The other night I dreamt that I died and went to heaven. This heaven was nothing like I expected. It was at the bottom of the sea. There were starfishes and mermaids all around me. The mermaids were dancing and singing in Latin like the priests do at the cathedral during Mass. You were there with me too, at the bottom of the sea. You were with your family, off to the side. Your father was acting like he was better than everyone else and he was standing in front of a sea cave blocking you from my view. I tried to talk to you, but every time I opened my mouth, water bubbles came out. No sounds.

they have this thing now that they do. if they come into a house and there is a son and mother there, they hold a gun to their heads. they make the son sleep with his mother. if it is a daughter and father, they do the same thing. some nights papa sleeps at his brother's, uncle pressoir's house. uncle pressoir sleeps at our house, just in case they come. that way papa will never be forced to lie down in bed with me. instead, uncle pressoir would be forced to, but that would not be as bad. we know a girl who had a child by her father that way. that is what papa does not want to happen, even if he is killed. there is still no gasoline to buy. otherwise we would be in ville rose already. papa has a friend who is going to get him some gasoline from a soldier. as soon as we get the gasoline, we are going to drive quick and fast until we find civilization. that's how papa puts it, civilization. he says things are not as bad in the provinces. i am still not talking to him. i don't think i ever will. manman says it is not his fault. he is trying to protect us. he cannot protect us. only god can protect us. the soldiers can come and do with us what they want. that makes papa feel weak, she says. he gets angry when he feels weak. why should he be angry with me? i am not one of the pigs with the machine guns. she asked me what really happened to you. she said she saw your parents before they left for the provinces. they did not want to tell her anything. i told her you took a boat after they raided the radio station, you escaped and took a boat to heaven knows where. she said, he was going to make a good man, that boy. sharp, like a needle point, that boy, he took the university exams a year before everyone else in this area. manman has respect for people with ambitions. she said papa did not want you for me because it did not seem as though you were going to do any better for me than he and manman could. he wants me to find a man who will do me some good. someone who will make sure that i have more than i have now. it is not enough for a girl to be just pretty anymore. we are not that well connected in society. the kind of man that papa wants for me would never have anything to do with me. all anyone can hope for is just a tiny bit of love, manman says, like a drop in a cup if you can get it, or a waterfall, a flood, if you can get that too. we do not have all that many high-up connections, she says, but you are an educated girl. what she counts for educated is not much to anyone but us anyway. they should be announcing the university exams on the radio next week. then i will know if you passed. i will listen for your name.

· ❀ ·

We spent most of yesterday telling stories. Someone says, Krik? You answer, Krak! And they say, I have many stories I could tell you, and then they go on and tell these stories to you, but mostly to themselves. Sometimes it feels like we have been at sea longer than the many years that I have been on this earth. The sun comes up and goes down. That is how you know it has been a whole day. I feel like we are sailing for Africa. Maybe we will go to Ginen, to live with the spirits, to be with everyone who has come and has died before us. They would probably turn us away from there too. Someone has a transistor and sometimes we listen to radio from the Bahamas. They treat Haitians like dogs in the Bahamas, a woman says. To them, we are not human. Even though their music sounds like ours. Their people look like ours. Even though we had the same African fathers who probably crossed these same seas together.

Do you want to know how people go to the bathroom on the boat? Probably the same way they did on those slaves ships years ago. They set aside a little corner for that. When I have to pee, I just pull it, lean over the rail, and do it very quickly. When I have to do the other thing, I rip a piece of something, squat down and do it, and throw the waste in the sea. I am always embarrassed by the smell. It is so demeaning having to squat in front of so many people. People turn away, but not always. At times I wonder if there is really land on the other side of the sea. Maybe the sea is endless. Like my love for you.

· ❈ ·

last night they came to madan roger's house. papa hurried inside as soon as madan roger's screaming started. the soldiers were looking for her son. madan roger was screaming, you killed him already. we buried his head. you can't kill him twice. they were shouting at her, do you belong to the youth federation with those vagabonds who were on the radio? she was yelling, do i look like a youth to you? can you identify your son's other associates? they asked her. papa had us tiptoe from the house into the latrine out back. we could hear it all from there. i thought i was going to choke on the smell of rotting poupou. they kept shouting at madan roger, did your son belong to the youth federation? wasn't he on the radio talking about the police? did he say, down with tonton macoutes? did he say, down with the army? he said that the military had to go; didn't he write slogans? he had meetings, didn't he? he demonstrated on the streets. you should have advised him better. she cursed on their mothers' graves. she just came out and shouted it, i hope your mothers will never rest in their cursed graves! she was just shouting it out, you killed him once already! you want to kill me too? go ahead. i don't care anymore. i'm dead already. you have already done the worst to me that you can do. you have killed my soul. they kept at it, asking her questions at the top of their voices: was your son a traitor? tell me all the names of his friends who were traitors just like him. madan roger finally shouts, yes, he was one! he belonged to that group. he was on the radio. he was on the streets at these demonstrations. he hated you like i hate you criminals. you killed him. they start to pound at her. you can hear it. you can hear the guns coming down on her head. it sounds like they are cracking all the bones in her body. manman whispers to papa, you can't just let them kill her. go and give them some money like you gave them for your daughter. papa says, the only money i have left is to get us out of here tomorrow. manman whispers, we cannot just stay here and let them kill her. manman starts moving like she is going out the door. papa grabs her neck and pins her to the latrine wall. tomorrow we are going to ville rose, he says. you will not spoil that for the family. you will not put us in that situation. you will not get us killed. going out there will be like trying to raise the dead. she is not dead yet, manman says, maybe we can help her. i will make you stay if i have to, he says to her. my mother buries her face in the latrine wall. she starts to cry. you can hear madan roger screaming. they are beating her, pounding on her until you don't hear anything else. manman tells papa, you cannot let them kill somebody just because you are afraid. papa says, oh yes, you *can* let them kill somebody because you are afraid. they are the law. it is their right. we are just being good citizens, following the law of the land. it has happened before all over this country and tonight it will happen again and there is nothing we can do.

· ❊ ·

Célianne spent the night groaning. She looks like she has been ready for a while, but maybe the child is being stubborn. She just screamed that she is bleeding. There is an older woman here who looks like she has had a lot of children herself. She says Célianne is not bleeding at all. Her water sack has broken.

The only babies I have ever seen right after birth are baby mice. Their skin looks veil thin. You can see all the blood vessels and all their organs. I have always wanted to poke them to see if my finger would go all the way through the skin.

I have moved to the other side of the boat so I will not have to look *inside* Célianne. People are just watching. The captain asks the midwife to keep Célianne steady so she will not rock any more holes into the boat. Now we have three cracks covered with tar. I am scared to think of what would happen if we had to choose among ourselves who would stay on the boat and who should die. Given the choice to make a decision like that, we would all act like vultures, including me.

The sun will set soon. Someone says that this child will be just another pair of hungry lips. At least it will have its mother's breasts, says an old man. Everyone will eat their last scraps of food today.

· ❧ ·

there is a rumor that the old president is coming back. there is a whole bunch of people going to the airport to meet him. papa says we are not going to stay in port-au-prince to find out if this is true or if it is a lie. they are selling gasoline at the market again. the carnival groups have taken to the streets. we are heading the other way, to ville rose. maybe there i will be able to sleep at night. it is not going to turn out well with the old president coming back, manman now says. people are just too hopeful, and sometimes hope is the biggest weapon of all to use against us. people will believe anything. they will claim to see the christ return and march on the cross backwards if there is enough hope. manman told papa that you took the boat. papa told me before we left this morning that he thought himself a bad father for everything that happened. he says a father should be able to speak to his children like a civilized man. all the craziness here has made him feel like he cannot do that anymore. all he wants to do is live. he and manman have not said a word to one another since we left the latrine. i know that papa does not hate us, not in the way that i hate those soldiers, those macoutes, and all those people here who shoot guns. on our way to ville rose, we saw dogs licking two dead faces. one of them was a little boy who was lying on the side of the road with the sun in his dead open eyes. we saw a soldier shoving a woman out of a hut, calling her a witch. he was shaving the woman's head, but of course we never stopped. papa didn't want to go in madan roger's house and check on her before we left. he thought the soldiers might still be there. papa was driving the van real fast. i thought he was going to kill us. we stopped at an open market on the way. manman got some black cloth for herself and for me. she cut the cloth in two pieces and we wrapped them around our heads to mourn madan roger. when i am used to ville rose, maybe i will sketch you some butterflies, depending on the news that they bring me.

· ❧ ·

Célianne had a girl baby. The woman acting as a midwife is holding the baby to the moon and whispering prayers . . . *God, this child You bring into the world, please guide her as You please through all her days on this earth.* The baby has not cried.

We had to throw our extra things in the sea because the water is beginning to creep in slowly. The boat needs to be lighter. My two gourdes in change had to be thrown overboard as an offering to Agwe, the spirit of the water. I heard the captain whisper to someone yesterday that they might have to *do something* with some of the people who never recovered from seasickness. I am afraid that soon they may ask me to throw out this notebook. We might all have to strip down to the way we were born, to keep ourselves from drowning.

Célianne's child is a beautiful child. They are calling her Swiss, because the word *Swiss* was written on the small knife they used to cut her umbilical cord. If she was my daughter, I would call her Soleil, Sun, Moon, or Star, after the elements. She still hasn't cried. There is gossip circulating about how Célianne became pregnant. Some people are saying that she had an affair with a married man and her parents threw her out. Gossip spreads here like everywhere else.

Do you remember our silly dreams? Passing the university exams and then studying hard to go until the end, the farthest of all that we can go in school. I know your father might never approve of me. I was going to try to win him over. He would have to cut out my heart to keep me from loving you. I hope you are writing like you promised. Jesus, Marie, Joseph! Everyone smells so bad. They get into arguments and they say to one another, "It is only my misfortune that would lump me together with an indigent like you." Think of it. They are fighting about being superior when we all might drown like straw.

There is an old toothless man leaning over to see what I am writing. He is sucking on the end of an old wooden pipe that has not seen any fire for a very long time now. He looks like a painting. Seeing things simply, you could fill a museum with the sights you have here. I still feel like such a coward for running away. Have you heard anything about my parents? Last time I saw them on the beach, my mother had a *kriz*. She just fainted on the sand. I saw her coming to as we started sailing away. But of course I don't know if she is doing all right.

The water is really piling into the boat. We take turns pouring bowls of it out. I don't know what is keeping the boat from splitting in two. Swiss isn't crying. They keep slapping her behind, but she is not crying.

· ❀ ·

of course the old president didn't come. they arrested a lot of people at the airport, shot a whole bunch of them down. i heard it on the radio. while we were eating tonight, i told papa that i love you. i don't know if it will make a difference. i just want him to know that i have loved somebody in my life. in case something happens to one of us, i think he should know this about me, that i have loved someone besides only my mother and father in my life. i know you would understand, you are the one for large noble gestures. i just wanted him to know that i was capable of loving somebody. he looked me straight in the eye and said nothing to me. i love you until my hair shivers at the thought of anything happening to you. papa just turned his face away like he was rejecting my very birth. i am writing you from under the banyan tree in the yard in our new house. there are only two rooms and a tin roof that makes music when it rains, especially when there is hail, which falls like angry tears from heaven. there is a stream down the hill from the house, a stream that is too shallow for me to drown myself. manman and i spend a lot of time talking under the banyan tree. she told me today that sometimes you have to choose between your father and the man you love. her whole family did not want her to marry papa because he was a gardener from ville rose and her family was from the city and some of them had even gone to university. she whispered everything under the banyan tree in the yard so as not to hurt his feelings. i saw him looking at us hard from the house. i heard him clearing his throat like he heard us anyway, like we hurt him very deeply somehow just by being together.

· ❧ ·

Célianne is lying with her head against the side of the boat. The baby still will not cry. They both look very peaceful in all this chaos. Célianne is holding her baby tight against her chest. She just cannot seem to let herself throw it in the ocean. I asked her about the baby's father. She keeps repeating the story now with her eyes closed, her lips barely moving.

She was home one night with her mother and brother Lionel when some ten or twelve soldiers burst into the house. The soldiers held a gun to Lionel's head and ordered him to lie down and become intimate with his mother. Lionel refused. Their mother told him to go ahead and obey the soldiers because she was afraid that they would kill Lionel on the spot if he put up more of a fight. Lionel did as his mother told him, crying as the soldiers laughed at him, pressing the gun barrels farther and farther into his neck.

Afterwards, the soldiers tied up Lionel and their mother, then they each took turns raping Célianne.

When they were done, they arrested Lionel, accusing him

of moral crimes. After that night, Célianne never heard from Lionel again.

The same night, Célianne cut her face with a razor so that no one would know who she was. Then as facial scars were healing, she started throwing up and getting rashes. Next thing she knew, she was getting big. She found out about the boat and got on. She is fifteen.

· ❧ ·

manman told me the whole story today under the banyan tree. the bastards were coming to get me. they were going to arrest me. they were going to peg me as a member of the youth federation and then take me away. papa heard about it. he went to the post and paid them money, all the money he had. our house in port-au-prince and all the land his father had left him, he gave it all away to save my life. this is why he was so mad. tonight manman told me this under the banyan tree. i have no words to thank him for this. i don't know how. you must love him for this, manman says, you must. it is something you can never forget, the sacrifice he has made. i cannot bring myself to say thank you. now he is more than my father. he is a man who gave everything he had to save my life. on the radio tonight, they read the list of names of people who passed the university exams. you passed.

· ❧ ·

We got some relief from the seawater coming in. The captain used the last of his tar, and most of the water is staying out for a while. Many people have volunteered to throw Céli-anne's baby overboard for her. She will not let them. They are waiting for her to go to sleep so they can do it, but she will not sleep. I never knew before that dead children looked purple. The lips are the most purple because the baby is so dark. Purple like the sea after the sun has set.

Célianne is slowly drifting off to sleep. She is very tired from the labor. I do not want to touch the child. If anybody is going to throw it in the ocean, I think it should be her. I keep thinking, they have thrown every piece of flesh that followed the child out of her body into the water. They are going to throw the dead baby in the water. Won't these things attract sharks?

Célianne's fingernails are buried deep in the child's naked back. The old man with the pipe just asked, "Konpè, what are you writing?" I told him, "My will."

· ❧ ·

i am getting used to ville rose. there are butterflies here, tons of butterflies. so far none has landed on my hand, which means they have no news for me. i cannot always bathe in the stream near the house because the water is freezing cold. the only time it feels just right is at noon, and then there are a dozen eyes who might see me bathing. i solved that by getting a bucket of water in the morning and leaving it in the sun and then bathing myself once it is night under the banyan tree. the banyan now is my most trusted friend. they say banyans can last hundreds of years. even the branches that lean down from them become like trees themselves. a banyan could become a forest, manman says, if it were given a chance. from the spot where i stand under the banyan, i see the mountains, and behind those are more mountains still. so many mountains that are bare like rocks. i feel like all those mountains are pushing me farther and farther away from you.

· ❖ ·

She threw it overboard. I watched her face knot up like a thread, and then she let go. It fell in a splash, floated for a while, and then sank. And quickly after that she jumped in too. And just as the baby's head sank, so did hers. They went together like two bottles beneath a waterfall. The shock lasts only so long. There was no time to even try and save her. There was no question of it. The sea in that spot is like the sharks that live there. It has no mercy.

They say I have to throw my notebook out. The old man has to throw out his hat and his pipe. The water is rising again and they are scooping it out. I asked for a few seconds to write this last page and then promised that I would let it go. I know you will probably never see this, but it was nice imagining that I had you here to talk to.

I hope my parents are alive. I asked the old man to tell them what happened to me, if he makes it anywhere. He asked me to write his name in "my book." I asked him for his full name. It is Justin Moïse André Nozius Joseph Frank Osnac Maximilien. He says it all with such an air that you would think him a king. The old man says, "I know a Coast Guard ship is coming. It came to me in my dream." He points to a spot far into the distance. I look where he is pointing. I see nothing. From here, ships must be like a mirage in the desert.

I must throw my book out now. It goes down to them, Célianne and her daughter and all those children of the sea who might soon be claiming me.

I go to them now as though it was always meant to be, as though the very day that my mother birthed me, she had chosen me to live life eternal, among the children of the deep blue sea, those who have escaped the chains of slavery to form a world beneath the heavens and the blood-drenched earth where you live.

Perhaps I was chosen from the beginning of time to live there with Agwe at the bottom of the sea. Maybe this is why I dreamed of the starfish and the mermaids having the Catholic Mass under the sea. Maybe this was my invitation to go. In any case, I know that my memory of you will live even there as I too become a child of the sea.

· ❖ ·

today i said thank you. i said thank you, papa, because you saved my life. he groaned and just touched my shoulder, moving his hand quickly away like a butterfly. and then there it was, the black butterfly floating around us. i began to run and run so it wouldn't land on me, but it had already carried its news. i know what must have happened. tonight i listened to manman's transistor under the banyan tree. all i hear from the radio is more killing in port-au-prince. the pigs are refusing to let up. i don't know what's going to happen, but i cannot see staying here forever. i am writing to you from the bottom of the banyan tree, manman says that banyan trees are holy and sometimes if we call the gods from beneath them, they will hear our voices clearer. now there are always butterflies around me, black ones that i refuse to let find my hand. i throw big rocks at them, but they are always too fast. last night on the radio, i heard that another boat sank off the coast of the bahamas. i can't think about you being in there in the waves. my hair shivers. from here, i cannot even see the sea. behind these mountains are more mountains and more black butterflies still and a sea that is endless like my love for you.

Nineteen Thirty-Seven

· ❀ ❀ ❀ ·

My Madonna cried. A miniature teardrop traveled down her white porcelain face, like dew on the tip of early morning grass. When I saw the tear I thought, surely, that my mother had died.

I sat motionless observing the Madonna the whole day. It did not shed another tear. I remained in the rocking chair until it was nightfall, my bones aching from the thought of another trip to the prison in Port-au-Prince. But, of course, I had to go.

The roads to the city were covered with sharp pebbles only half buried in the thick dust. I chose to go barefoot, as my mother had always done on her visits to the Massacre River, the river separating Haiti from the Spanish-speaking country that she had never allowed me to name because I had been born on the night that El Generalissimo, Dios Trujillo, the honorable chief of state, had ordered the massacre of all Haitians living there.

The sun was just rising when I got to the capital. The first city person I saw was an old woman carrying a jar full of leeches. Her gaze was glued to the Madonna tucked under my arm.

"May I see it?" she asked.

I held out the small statue that had been owned by my family ever since it was given to my great-great-great-grandmother Défilé by a French man who had kept her as a slave.

The old woman's index finger trembled as it moved toward the Madonna's head. She closed her eyes at the moment of contact, her wrists shaking.

"Where are you from?" she asked. She had layers of 'respectable' wrinkles on her face, the kind my mother might also have one day, if she has a chance to survive.

"I am from Ville Rose," I said, "the city of painters and poets, the coffee city, with beaches where the sand is either black or white, but never mixed together, where the fields are endless and sometimes the cows are yellow like cornmeal."

The woman put the jar of leeches under her arm to keep them out of the sun.

"You're here to see a prisoner?" she asked.

"Yes."

"I know where you can buy some very good food for this person."

She led me by the hand to a small alley where a girl was selling fried pork and plantains wrapped in brown paper. I bought some meat for my mother after asking the cook to fry it once more and then sprinkle it with spiced cabbage.

The yellow prison building was like a fort, as large and strong as in the days when it was used by the American marines who had built it. The Americans taught us how to build prisons. By the end of the 1915 occupation, the police in the city really knew how to hold human beings trapped in cages, even women like Manman who was accused of having wings of flame.

The prison yard was as quiet as a cave when a young Haitian guard escorted me there to wait. The smell of the fried pork mixed with that of urine and excrement was almost unbearable. I sat on a pile of bricks, trying to keep the Madonna from sliding through my fingers. I dug my buttocks farther into the bricks, hoping perhaps that my body might sink down to the ground and disappear before my mother emerged as a ghost to greet me.

The other prisoners had not yet woken up. All the better, for I did not want to see them, these bone-thin women with shorn heads, carrying clumps of their hair in their bare hands, as they sought the few rays of sunshine that they were allowed each day.

My mother had grown even thinner since the last time I had seen her. Her face looked like the gray of a late evening sky. These days, her skin barely clung to her bones, falling in layers, flaps, on her face and neck. The prison guards watched her more closely because they thought that the wrinkles resulted from her taking off her skin at night and then putting it back on in a hurry, before sunrise. This was why Manman's sentence had been extended to life. And when she died, her remains were to be burnt in the prison yard, to prevent her spirit from wandering into any young innocent bodies.

I held out the fried pork and plantains to her. She uncovered the food and took a peek before grimacing, as though the sight of the meat nauseated her. Still she took it and put it in a deep pocket in a very loose fitting white dress that she had made herself from the cloth that I had brought her on my last visit.

I said nothing. Ever since the morning of her arrest, I had not been able to say anything to her. It was as though I became mute the moment I stepped into the prison yard. Sometimes I wanted to speak, yet I was not able to open my mouth or raise my tongue. I wondered if she saw my struggle in my eyes.

She pointed at the Madonna in my hands, opening her arms to receive it. I quickly handed her the statue. She smiled. Her teeth were a dark red, as though caked with blood from the initial beating during her arrest. At times, she seemed happier to see the Madonna than she was to see me.

She rubbed the space under the Madonna's eyes, then tasted her fingertips, the way a person tests for salt in salt water.

"Has she cried?" Her voice was hoarse from lack of use. With every visit, it seemed to get worse and worse. I was afraid that one day, like me, she would not be able to say anything at all.

I nodded, raising my index finger to show that the Madonna had cried a single tear. She pressed the statue against her chest as if to reward the Madonna and then, suddenly, broke down and began sobbing herself.

I reached over and patted her back, the way one burps a baby. She continued to sob until a guard came and nudged her, poking the barrel of his rifle into her side. She raised her head, keeping the Madonna lodged against her chest as she forced a brave smile.

"They have not treated me badly," she said. She smoothed her hands over her bald head, from her forehead to the back of her neck. The guards shaved her head every week. And before the women went to sleep, the guards made them throw tin cups of cold water at one another so that their bodies would not be able to muster up enough heat to grow those wings made of flames, fly away in the middle of the night, slip into the slumber of innocent children and steal their breath.

Manman pulled the meat and plantains out of her pocket and started eating a piece to fill the silence. Her normal ration of food in the prison was bread and water, which is why she was losing weight so rapidly.

"Sometimes the food you bring me, it lasts for months at a time," she said. "I chew it and swallow my saliva, then I put it away and then chew it again. It lasts a very long time this way."

A few of the other women prisoners walked out into the yard, their chins nearly touching their chests, their shaved heads sunk low on bowed necks. Some had large boils on their heads. One, drawn by the fresh smell of fried pork, came to sit near us and began pulling the scabs from the bruises on her scalp, a line of blood dripping down her back.

All of these women were here for the same reason. They were said to have been seen at night rising from the ground like birds on fire. A loved one, a friend, or a neighbor had accused them of causing the death of a child. A few other people agreeing with these stories was all that was needed to have them arrested. And sometimes even killed.

I remembered so clearly the day Manman was arrested. We were new to the city and had been sleeping on a cot at a friend's house. The friend had a sick baby who was suffering with colic. Every once in a while, Manman would wake up to look after the child when the mother was so tired that she no longer heard her son's cries.

One morning when I woke up, Manman was gone. There was the sound of a crowd outside. When I rushed out I saw a group of people taking my mother away. Her face was bleeding from the pounding blows of rocks and sticks and the fists of strangers. She was being pulled along by two policemen, each tugging at one of her arms as she dragged her feet. The woman we had been staying with carried her dead son by the legs. The policemen made no efforts to stop the mob that was beating my mother.

"*Lougawou,* witch, criminal!" they shouted.

I dashed into the street, trying to free Manman from the crowd. I wasn't even able to get near her.

I followed her cries to the prison. Her face was swollen to three times the size that it had been. She had to drag herself across the clay floor on her belly when I saw her in the prison cell. She was like a snake, someone with no bones left in her body. I was there watching when they shaved her head for the first time. At first I thought they were doing it so that the open gashes on her scalp could heal. Later, when I saw all the other women in the yard, I realized that they wanted to make them look like crows, like men.

Now, Manman sat with the Madonna pressed against her chest, her eyes staring ahead, as though she was looking into the future. She had never talked very much about the future. She had always believed more in the past.

When I was five years old, we went on a pilgrimage to the Massacre River, which I had expected to be still crimson with blood, but which was as clear as any water that I had ever seen. Manman had taken my hand and pushed it into the river, no farther than my wrist. When we dipped our hands, I thought that the dead would reach out and haul us in, but only our own faces stared back at us, one indistinguishable from the other.

With our hands in the water, Manman spoke to the sun. "Here is my child, Josephine. We were saved from the tomb of this river when she was still in my womb. You spared us both, her and me, from this river where I lost my mother."

My mother had escaped El Generalissimo's soldiers, leaving her own mother behind. From the Haitian side of the river, she could still see the soldiers chopping up *her* mother's body and throwing it into the river along with many others.

We went to the river many times as I was growing up. Every year my mother would invite a few more women who had also lost their mothers there.

Until we moved to the city, we went to the river every year on the first of November. The women would all dress in white. My mother would hold my hand tightly as we walked toward the water. We were all daughters of that river, which had taken our mothers from us. Our mothers were the ashes and we were the light. Our mothers were the embers and we were the sparks. Our mothers were the flames and we were the blaze. We came from the bottom of that river where the blood never stops flowing, where my mother's dive toward life—her swim among all those bodies slaughtered in flight— gave her those wings of flames. The river was the place where it had all begun.

"At least I gave birth to my daughter on the night that my mother was taken from me," she would say. "At least you came out at the right moment to take my mother's place."

· ❈ ·

Now in the prison yard, my mother was trying to avoid the eyes of the guard peering down at her.

"One day I will tell you the secret of how the Madonna cries," she said.

I reached over and touched the scabs on her fingers. She handed me back the Madonna.

I know how the Madonna cries. I have watched while hiding how my mother plans weeks in advance for it to happen. She would put a thin layer of wax and oil in the hollow space of the Madonna's eyes and when the wax melted, the oil would roll down the little face shedding a more perfect tear than either she or I could ever cry.

"You go. Let me watch you leave," she said, sitting stiffly.

I kissed her on the cheek and tried to embrace her, but she quickly pushed me away.

"You will please visit me again soon," she said.

I nodded my head yes.

"Let your flight be joyful," she said, "and mine too."

I nodded and then ran out of the yard, fleeing before I could flood the front of my dress with my tears. There had been too much crying already.

· ❈ ·

Manman had a cough the next time I visited her. She sat in a corner of the yard, and as she trembled in the sun, she clung to the Madonna.

"The sun can no longer warm God's creatures," she said. "What has this world come to when the sun can no longer warm God's creatures?"

I wanted to wrap my body around hers, but I knew she would not let me.

"God only knows what I have got under my skin from being here. I may die of tuberculosis, or perhaps there are worms right now eating me inside."

· ❧ ·

When I went again, I decided that I would talk. Even if the words made no sense, I would try to say something to her. But before I could even say hello, she was crying. When I handed her the Madonna, she did not want to take it. The guard was looking directly at us. Manman still had a fever that made her body tremble. Her eyes had the look of delirium.

"Keep the Madonna when I am gone," she said. "When I am completely gone, maybe you will have someone to take my place. Maybe you will have a person. Maybe you will have *some flesh* to console you. But if you don't, you will always have the Madonna."

"Manman, did you fly?" I asked her.

She did not even blink at my implied accusation.

"Oh, now you talk," she said, "when I am nearly gone. Perhaps you don't remember. All the women who came with us to the river, they could go to the moon and back if that is what they wanted."

· ❖ ·

A week later, almost to the same day, an old woman stopped by my house in Ville Rose on her way to Port-au-Prince. She came in the middle of the night, wearing the same white dress that the women usually wore on their trips to dip their hands in the river.

"Sister," the old woman said from the doorway. "I have come for you."

"I don't know you," I said.

"You *do* know me," she said. "My name is Jacqueline. I have been to the river with you."

I had been by the river with many people. I remembered a Jacqueline who went on the trips with us, but I was not sure this was the same woman. If she were really from the river, she would know. She would know all the things that my mother had said to the sun as we sat with our hands dipped in the water, questioning each other, making up codes and disciplines by which we could always know who the other daughters of the river were.

"Who are you?" I asked her.

"I am a child of that place," she answered. "I come from that long trail of blood."

"Where are you going?"

"I am walking into the dawn."

"Who are you?"

"I am the first daughter of the first star."

"Where do you drink when you're thirsty?"

"I drink the tears from the Madonna's eyes."

"And if not there?"

"I drink the dew."

"And if you can't find dew?"

"I drink from the rain before it falls."

"If you can't drink there?"

"I drink from the turtle's hide."

"How did you find your way to me?"

"By the light of the mermaid's comb."

"Where does your mother come from?"

"Thunderbolts, lightning, and all things that soar."

"Who are you?"

"I am the flame and the spark by which my mother lived."

"Where do you come from?"

"I come from the puddle of that river."

"Speak to me."

"You hear my mother who speaks through me. She is the shadow that follows my shadow. The flame at the tip of my candle. The ripple in the stream where I wash my face. Yes. I will eat my tongue if ever I whisper that name, the name of that place across the river that took my mother from me."

I knew then that she had been with us, for she knew all the answers to the questions I asked.

"I think you do know who I am," she said, staring deeply into the pupils of my eyes. "I know who *you* are. You are Josephine. And your mother knew how to make the Madonna cry."

I let Jacqueline into the house. I offered her a seat in the rocking chair, gave her a piece of hard bread and a cup of cold coffee.

"Sister, I do not want to be the one to tell you," she said, "but your mother is dead. If she is not dead now, then she will be when we get to Port-au-Prince. Her blood calls to me from the ground. Will you go with me to see her? Let us go to see her."

We took a mule for most of the trip. Jacqueline was not strong enough to make the whole journey on foot. I brought the Madonna with me, and Jacqueline took a small bundle with some black rags in it.

When we got to the city, we went directly to the prison gates. Jacqueline whispered Manman's name to a guard and waited for a response.

"She will be ready for burning this afternoon," the guard said.

My blood froze inside me. I lowered my head as the news sank in.

"Surely, it is not that much a surprise," Jacqueline said, stroking my shoulder. She had become rejuvenated, as though strengthened by the correctness of her prediction.

"We only want to visit her cell," Jacqueline said to the guard. "We hope to take her personal things away."

The guard seemed too tired to argue, or perhaps he saw in Jacqueline's face traces of some long-dead female relative whom he had not done enough to please while she was still alive.

He took us to the cell where my mother had spent the last year. Jacqueline entered first, and then I followed. The room felt damp, the clay breaking into small muddy chunks under our feet.

I inhaled deeply to keep my lungs from aching. Jacqueline

said nothing as she carefully walked around the women who sat like statues in different corners of the cell. There were six of them. They kept their arms close to their bodies, like angels hiding their wings. In the middle of the cell was an arrangement of sand and pebbles in the shape of a cross for my mother. Each woman was either wearing or holding something that had belonged to her.

One of them clutched a pillow as she stared at the Madonna. The woman was wearing my mother's dress, the large white dress that had become like a tent on Manman.

I walked over to her and asked, "What happened?"

"Beaten down in the middle of the yard," she whispered.

"Like a dog," said another woman.

"Her skin, it was too loose," said the woman wearing my mother's dress. "They said prison could not cure her."

The woman reached inside my mother's dress pocket and pulled out a handful of chewed pork and handed it to me. I motioned her hand away.

"No no, I would rather not."

She then gave me the pillow, my mother's pillow. It was open, half filled with my mother's hair. Each time they shaved her head, my mother had kept the hair for her pillow. I hugged the pillow against my chest, feeling some of the hair rising in clouds of dark dust into my nostrils.

Jacqueline took a long piece of black cloth out of her bundle and wrapped it around her belly.

"Sister," she said, "life is never lost, another one always comes up to replace the last. Will you come watch when they burn the body?"

"What would be the use?" I said.

"They will make these women watch, and we can keep them company."

When Jacqueline took my hand, her fingers felt balmy and warm against the lifelines in my palm. For a brief second, I saw nothing but black. And then I *saw* the crystal glow of the river as we had seen it every year when my mother dipped my hand in it.

"I would go," I said, "if I knew the truth, whether a woman can fly."

"Why did you not ever ask your mother," Jacqueline said, "if she knew how to fly?"

Then the story came back to me as my mother had often told it. On that day so long ago, in the year nineteen hundred and thirty-seven, in the Massacre River, my mother did fly. Weighted down by my body inside hers, she leaped from Dominican soil into the water, and out again on the Haitian side of the river. She glowed red when she came out, blood clinging to her skin, which at that moment looked as though it were in flames.

In the prison yard, I held the Madonna tightly against my chest, so close that I could smell my mother's scent on the statue. When Jacqueline and I stepped out into the yard to wait for the burning, I raised my head toward the sun thinking, One day I may just see my mother there.

"Let her flight be joyful," I said to Jacqueline. "And mine and yours too."

A Wall of Fire Rising

· ❖ ❖ ❖ ·

· ❀ ❀ ❀ ·

"Listen to what happened today," Guy said as he barged through the rattling door of his tiny shack.

His wife, Lili, was squatting in the middle of their one-room home, spreading cornmeal mush on banana leaves for their supper.

"Listen to what happened to *me* today!" Guy's seven-year-old son—Little Guy—dashed from a corner and grabbed his father's hand. The boy dropped his composition notebook as he leaped to his father, nearly stepping into the corn mush and herring that his mother had set out in a trio of half gourds on the clay floor.

"Our boy is in a play." Lili quickly robbed Little Guy of the honor of telling his father the news.

"A play?" Guy affectionately stroked the boy's hair.

The boy had such tiny corkscrew curls that no amount of brushing could ever make them all look like a single entity. The other boys at the Lycee Jean-Jacques called him "pepper head" because each separate kinky strand was coiled into a tight tiny ball that looked like small peppercorns.

"When is this play?" Guy asked both the boy and his wife. "Are we going to have to buy new clothes for this?"

Lili got up from the floor and inclined her face towards her husband's in order to receive her nightly peck on the cheek.

"What role do you have in the play?" Guy asked, slowly rubbing the tip of his nails across the boy's scalp. His fingers made a soft grating noise with each invisible circle drawn around the perimeters of the boy's head. Guy's fingers finally landed inside the boy's ears, forcing the boy to giggle until he almost gave himself the hiccups.

"Tell me, what is your part in the play?" Guy asked again, pulling his fingers away from his son's ear.

"I am Boukman," the boy huffed out, as though there was some laughter caught in his throat.

"Show Papi your lines," Lili told the boy as she arranged the three open gourds on a piece of plywood raised like a table on two bricks, in the middle of the room. "My love, Boukman is the hero of the play."

The boy went back to the corner where he had been studying and pulled out a thick book carefully covered in brown paper.

"You're going to spend a lifetime learning those." Guy took the book from the boy's hand and flipped through the pages quickly. He had to strain his eyes to see the words by the light of an old kerosene lamp, which that night—like all others—flickered as though it was burning its very last wick.

"All these words seem so long and heavy," Guy said. "You think you can do this, son?"

"He has one very good speech," Lili said. "Page forty, remember, son?"

The boy took back the book from his father. His face was crimped in an of-course-I-remember look as he searched for page forty.

"Bouk-man," Guy struggled with the letters of the slave revolutionary's name as he looked over his son's shoulders. "I see some very hard words here, son."

"He already knows his speech," Lili told her husband.

"Does he now?" asked Guy.

"We've been at it all afternoon," Lili said. "Why don't you go on and recite that speech for your father?"

The boy tipped his head towards the rusting tin on the roof as he prepared to recite his lines.

Lili wiped her hands on an old apron tied around her waist and stopped to listen.

"Remember what you are," Lili said, "a great rebel leader. Remember, it is the revolution."

"Do we want him to be all of that?" Guy asked.

"He is Boukman," Lili said. "What is the only thing on your mind now, Boukman?"

"Supper," Guy whispered, enviously eyeing the food cooling off in the middle of the room. He and the boy looked at each other and began to snicker.

"Tell us the other thing that is on your mind," Lili said, joining in their laughter.

"Freedom!" shouted the boy, as he quickly slipped into his role.

"Louder!" urged Lili.

"Freedom is on my mind!" yelled the boy.

"Why don't you start, son?" said Guy. "If you don't, we'll never get to that other thing that we have on our minds."

The boy closed his eyes and took a deep breath. At first, his lips parted but nothing came out. Lili pushed her head forward as though she were holding her breath. Then like the last burst of lightning out of clearing sky, the boy began.

"A wall of fire is rising and in the ashes, I see the bones of my people. Not only those people whose dark hollow faces I see daily in the fields, but all those souls who have gone ahead to haunt my dreams. At night I relive once more the last caresses from the hand of a loving father, a valiant love, a beloved friend."

It was obvious that this was a speech written by a European man, who gave to the slave revolutionary Boukman the kind of European phrasing that might have sent the real Boukman turning in his grave. However, the speech made Lili and Guy stand on the tips of their toes from great pride. As their applause thundered in the small space of their shack that night, they felt as though for a moment they had been given the rare pleasure of hearing the voice of one of the forefathers of Haitian independence in the forced baritone of their only child. The experience left them both with a strange feeling that they could not explain. It left the hair on the back of their necks standing on end. It left them feeling much more love than they ever knew that they could add to their feeling for their son.

"Bravo," Lili cheered, pressing her son into the folds of her apron. "Long live Boukman and long live my boy."

"Long live our supper," Guy said, quickly batting his eyelashes to keep tears from rolling down his face.

· ❃ ·

The boy kept his eyes on his book as they ate their supper that night. Usually Guy and Lili would not have allowed that, but this was a special occasion. They watched proudly as the boy muttered his lines between swallows of cornmeal.

The boy was still mumbling the same words as the three of them used the last of the rainwater trapped in old gasoline containers and sugarcane pulp from the nearby sugarcane mill to scrub the calabashes that they had eaten from.

When things were really bad for the family, they boiled clean sugarcane pulp to make what Lili called her special sweet water tea. It was supposed to suppress gas and kill the vermin in the stomach that made poor children hungry. That and a pinch of salt under the tongue could usually quench hunger until Guy found a day's work or Lili could manage to buy spices on credit and then peddle them for a profit at the marketplace.

That night, anyway, things were good. Everyone had eaten enough to put all their hunger vermin to sleep.

The boy was sitting in front of the shack on an old plastic bucket turned upside down, straining his eyes to find the words on the page. Sometimes when there was no kerosene for the lamp, the boy would have to go sit by the side of the road and study under the street lamps with the rest of the neighborhood children. Tonight, at least, they had a bit of their own light.

Guy bent down by a small clump of old mushrooms near the boy's feet, trying to get a better look at the plant. He emptied the last drops of rainwater from a gasoline container on the mushroom, wetting the bulging toes sticking out of his sons' sandals, which were already coming apart around his endlessly growing feet.

Guy tried to pluck some of the mushrooms, which were

being pushed into the dust as though they wanted to grow beneath the ground as roots. He took one of the mushrooms in his hand, running his smallest finger over the round bulb. He clipped the stem and buried the top in a thick strand of his wife's hair.

The mushroom looked like a dried insect in Lili's hair.

"It sure makes you look special," Guy said, teasing her.

"Thank you so much," Lili said, tapping her husband's arm. "It's nice to know that I deserve these much more than roses."

Taking his wife's hand, Guy said, "Let's go to the sugar mill."

"Can I study my lines there?" the boy asked.

"You know them well enough already," Guy said.

"I need many repetitions," the boy said.

· ❧ ·

Their feet sounded as though they were playing a wet wind instrument as they slipped in and out of the puddles between the shacks in the shantytown. Near the sugar mill was a large television screen in an iron grill cage that the government had installed so that the shantytown dwellers could watch the state-sponsored news at eight o'clock every night. After the news, a gendarme would come and turn off the television set, taking home the key. On most nights, the people stayed at the site long after this gendarme had gone and told stories to one another beneath the big blank screen. They made bonfires with dried sticks, corn husks, and paper, cursing the authorities under their breath.

There was a crowd already gathering for the nightly news

event. The sugar mill workers sat in the front row in chairs or on old buckets.

Lili and Guy passed the group, clinging to their son so that in his childhood naïveté he wouldn't accidentally glance at the wrong person and be called an insolent child. They didn't like the ambiance of the nightly news watch. They spared themselves trouble by going instead to the sugar mill, where in the past year they had discovered their own wonder.

Everyone knew that the family who owned the sugar mill were eccentric "Arabs," Haitians of Lebanese or Palestinian descent whose family had been in the country for generations. The Assad family had a son who, it seems, was into all manner of odd things, the most recent of which was a hot-air balloon, which he had brought to Haiti from America and occasionally flew over the shantytown skies.

As they approached the fence surrounding the field where the large wicker basket and deflated balloon rested on the ground, Guy let go of the hands of both his wife and the boy.

Lili walked on slowly with her son. For the last few weeks, she had been feeling as though Guy was lost to her each time he reached this point, twelve feet away from the balloon. As Guy pushed his hand through the barbed wire, she could tell from the look on his face that he was thinking of sitting inside the square basket while the smooth rainbow surface of the balloon itself floated above his head. During the day, when the field was open, Guy would walk up to the basket, staring at it with the same kind of longing that most men display when they admire very pretty girls.

Lili and the boy stood watching from a distance as Guy tried to push his hand deeper, beyond the chain link fence that separated him from the balloon. He reached into his pants pocket and pulled out a small pocketknife, sharpening the edges on the metal surface of the fence. When his wife and child moved closer, he put the knife back in his pocket, letting his fingers slide across his son's tightly coiled curls.

"I wager you I can make this thing fly," Guy said.

"Why do you think you can do that?" Lili asked.

"I know it," Guy replied.

He followed her as she circled the sugar mill, leading to their favorite spot under a watch light. Little Guy lagged faithfully behind them. From this distance, the hot-air balloon looked like an odd spaceship.

Lili stretched her body out in the knee-high grass in the field. Guy reached over and tried to touch her between her legs.

"You're not one to worry, Lili," he said. "You're not afraid of the frogs, lizards, or snakes that could be hiding in this grass?"

"I am here with my husband," she said. "You are here to protect me if anything happens."

Guy reached into his shirt pocket and pulled out a lighter and a crumpled piece of paper. He lit the paper until it burned to an ashy film. The burning paper floated in the night breeze for a while, landing in fragments on the grass.

"Did you see that, Lili?" Guy asked with a flame in his eyes brighter than the lighter's. "Did you see how the paper floated when it was burned? This is how that balloon flies."

"What did you mean by saying that you could make it fly?" Lili asked.

"You already know all my secrets," Guy said as the boy came charging towards them.

"Papa, could you play *lago* with me?" the boy asked.

Lili lay peacefully on the grass as her son and husband played hide-and-seek. Guy kept hiding and his son kept finding him as each time Guy made it easier for the boy.

"We rest now." Guy was becoming breathless.

The stars were circling the peaks of the mountains, dipping into the cane fields belonging to the sugar mill. As Guy caught his breath, the boy raced around the fence, running as fast as he could to purposely make himself dizzy.

"Listen to what happened today," Guy whispered softly in Lili's ear.

"I heard you say that when you walked in the house tonight," Lili said. "With the boy's play, I forgot to ask you."

The boy sneaked up behind them, his face lit up, though his brain was spinning. He wrapped his arms around both their necks.

"We will go back home soon," Lili said.

"Can I recite my lines?" asked the boy.

"We have heard them," Guy said. "Don't tire your lips."

The boy mumbled something under his breath. Guy grabbed his ear and twirled it until it was a tiny ball in his hand. The boy's face contorted with agony as Guy made him kneel in the deep grass in punishment.

Lili looked tortured as she watched the boy squirming in the grass, obviously terrified of the crickets, lizards, and small snakes that might be there.

"Perhaps we should take him home to bed," she said.

"He will never learn," Guy said, "if I say one thing and you say another."

Guy got up and angrily started walking home. Lili walked over, took her son's hand, and raised him from his knees.

"You know you must not mumble," she said.

"I was saying my lines," the boy said.

"Next time say them loud," Lili said, "so he knows what is coming out of your mouth."

That night Lili could hear her son muttering his lines as he tucked himself in his corner of the room and drifted off to sleep. The boy still had the book with his monologue in it clasped under his arm as he slept.

· ❧ ·

Guy stayed outside in front of the shack as Lili undressed for bed. She loosened the ribbon that held the old light blue cotton skirt around her waist and let it drop past her knees. She grabbed half a lemon that she kept in the corner by the folded mat that she and Guy unrolled to sleep on every night. Lili let her blouse drop to the floor as she smoothed the lemon over her ashen legs.

Guy came in just at that moment and saw her bare chest by the light of the smaller castor oil lamp that they used for the later hours of the night. Her skin had coarsened a bit over the years, he thought. Her breasts now drooped from having nursed their son for two years after he was born. It was now easier for him to imagine their son's lips around those breasts than to imagine his anywhere near them.

He turned his face away as she fumbled for her nightgown. He helped her open the mat, tucking the blanket edges underneath.

Fully clothed, Guy dropped onto the mat next to her. He laid his head on her chest, rubbing the spiky edges of his hair against her nipples.

"What was it that happened today?" Lili asked, running her fingers along Guy's hairline, an angular hairline, almost like a triangle, in the middle of his forehead. She nearly didn't marry him because it was said that people with angular hairlines often have very troubled lives.

"I got a few hours' work for tomorrow at the sugar mill," Guy said. "That's what happened today."

"It was such a long time coming," Lili said.

It was almost six months since the last time Guy had gotten work there. The jobs at the sugar mill were few and far between. The people who had them never left, or when they did they would pass the job on to another family member who was already waiting on line.

Guy did not seem overjoyed about the one day's work.

"I wish I had paid more attention when you came in with the news," Lili said. "I was just so happy about the boy."

"I was born in the shadow of that sugar mill," Guy said. "Probably the first thing my mother gave me to drink as a baby was some sweet water tea from the pulp of the sugarcane. If anyone deserves to work there, I should."

"What will you be doing for your day's work?"

"Would you really like to know?"

"There is never any shame in honest work," she said.

"They want me to scrub the latrines."

"It's honest work," Lili said, trying to console him.

"I am still number seventy-eight on the permanent hire list," he said. "I was thinking of putting the boy on the list now, so maybe by the time he becomes a man he can be up for a job."

Lili's body jerked forward, rising straight up in the air. Guy's head dropped with a loud thump onto the mat.

"I don't want him on that list," she said. "For a young boy to be on any list like that might influence his destiny. I don't want him on the list."

"Look at me," Guy said. "If my father had worked there, if he had me on the list, don't you think I would be working?"

"If you have any regard for me," she said, "you will not put him on the list."

She groped for her husband's chest in the dark and laid her head on it. She could hear his heart beating loudly as though it were pumping double, triple its normal rate.

"You won't put the boy on any lists, will you?" she implored.

"Please, Lili, no more about the boy. He will not go on the list."

"Thank you."

"Tonight I was looking at that balloon in the yard behind the sugar mill," he said. "I have been watching it real close."

"I know."

"I have seen the man who owns it," he said. "I've seen him get in it and put it in the sky and go up there like it was some kind of kite and he was the kite master. I see the men who run after it trying to figure out where it will land. Once I was there and I was one of those men who were running and I actually guessed correctly. I picked a spot in the cleared sugarcane fields. I picked the spot from a distance and it actually landed there."

"Let me say something to you, Guy—"

"Pretend that this is the time of miracles and we believed in them. I watched the owner for a long time, and I think I can fly that balloon. The first time I saw him do it, it looked like a miracle, but the more and more I saw it, the more ordinary it became."

"You're probably intelligent enough to do it," she said.

"I am intelligent enough to do it. You're right to say that I can."

"Don't you think about hurting yourself?"

"Think like this. Can't you see yourself up there? Up in the clouds somewhere like some kind of bird?"

"If God wanted people to fly, he would have given us wings on our backs."

"You're right, Lili, you're right. But look what he gave us instead. He gave us reasons to want to fly. He gave us the air, the birds, our son."

"I don't understand you," she said.

"Our son, your son, you do not want him cleaning latrines."

"He can do other things."

"Me too. I can do other things too."

A loud scream came from the corner where the boy was sleeping. Lili and Guy rushed to him and tried to wake him. The boy was trembling when he opened his eyes.

"What is the matter?" Guy asked.

"I cannot remember my lines," the boy said.

Lili tried to string together what she could remember of her son's lines. The words slowly came back to the boy. By the time he fell back to sleep, it was almost dawn.

· ❀ ·

The light was slowly coming up behind the trees. Lili could hear the whispers of the market women, their hisses and swearing as their sandals dug into the sharp-edged rocks on the road.

She turned her back to her husband as she slipped out of her nightgown, quickly putting on her day clothes.

"Imagine this," Guy said from the mat on the floor. "I have never really seen your entire body in broad daylight."

Lili shut the door behind her, making her way out to the yard. The empty gasoline containers rested easily on her head as she walked a few miles to the public water fountains. It was harder to keep them steady when the containers were full. The water splashed all over her blouse and rippled down her back.

The sky was blue as it was most mornings, a dark indigo-shaded turquoise that would get lighter when the sun was fully risen.

Guy and the boy were standing in the yard waiting for her when she got back.

"You did not get much sleep, my handsome boy," she said, running her wet fingers over the boy's face.

"He'll be late for school if we do not go right now," Guy said. "I want to drop him off before I start work."

"Do we remember our lines this morning?" Lili asked, tucking the boy's shirt down deep into his short pants.

"We just recited them," Guy said. "Even I know them now."

Lili watched them walk down the footpath, her eyes following them until they disappeared.

As soon as they were out of sight, she poured the water she had fetched into a large calabash, letting it stand beside the house.

She went back into the room and slipped into a dry blouse. It was never too early to start looking around, to scrape together that night's meal.

· ❧ ·

"Listen to what happened again today," Lili said when Guy walked through the door that afternoon.

Guy blotted his face with a dust rag as he prepared to hear the news. After the day he'd had at the factory, he wanted to sit under a tree and have a leisurely smoke, but he did not want to set a bad example for his son by indulging his very small pleasures.

"You tell him, son," Lili urged the boy, who was quietly sitting in a corner, reading.

"I've got more lines," the boy announced, springing up to his feet. "Papi, do you want to hear them?"

"They are giving him more things to say in the play," Lili explained, "because he did such a good job memorizing so fast."

"My compliments, son. Do you have your new lines memorized too?" Guy asked.

"Why don't you recite your new lines for your father?" Lili said.

The boy walked to the middle of the room and prepared to recite. He cleared his throat, raising his eyes towards the ceiling.

"There is so much sadness in the faces of my people. I have called on their gods, now I call on our gods. I call on our young. I call on our old. I call on our mighty and the weak. I call on everyone and anyone so that we shall all let

out one piercing cry that we may either live freely or we should die."

"I see your new lines have as much drama as the old ones," Guy said. He wiped a tear away, walked over to the chair, and took the boy in his arms. He pressed the boy's body against his chest before lowering him to the ground.

"Your new lines are wonderful, son. They're every bit as affecting as the old." He tapped the boy's shoulder and walked out of the house.

"What's the matter with Papi?" the boy asked as the door slammed shut behind Guy.

"His heart hurts," Lili said.

· ❧ ·

After supper, Lili took her son to the field where she knew her husband would be. While the boy ran around, she found her husband sitting in his favorite spot behind the sugar mill.

"Nothing, Lili," he said. "Ask me nothing about this day that I have had."

She sat down on the grass next to him, for once feeling the sharp edges of the grass blades against her ankles.

"You're really good with that boy," he said, drawing circles with his smallest finger on her elbow. "You will make a performer of him. I know you will. You can see the best in that whole situation. It's because you have those stars in your eyes. That's the first thing I noticed about you when I met you. It was your eyes, Lili, so dark and deep. They drew me like danger draws a fool."

He turned over on the grass so that he was staring directly

at the moon up in the sky. She could tell that he was also watching the hot-air balloon behind the sugar mill fence out of the corner of his eye.

"Sometimes I know you want to believe in me," he said. "I know you're wishing things for me. You want me to work at the mill. You want me to get a pretty house for us. I know you want these things too, but mostly you want me to feel like a man. That's why you're not one to worry about, Lili. I know you can take things as they come."

"I don't like it when you talk this way," she said.

"Listen to this, Lili. I want to tell you a secret. Sometimes, I just want to take that big balloon and ride it up in the air. I'd like to sail off somewhere and keep floating until I got to a really nice place with a nice plot of land where I could be something new. I'd build my own house, keep my own garden. Just *be* something new."

"I want you to stay away from there."

"I know you don't think I should take it. That can't keep me from wanting."

"You could be injured. Do you ever think about that?"

"Don't you ever want to be something new?"

"I don't like it," she said.

"Please don't get angry with me," he said, his voice straining almost like the boy's.

"If you were to take that balloon and fly away, would you take me and the boy?"

"First you don't want me to take it and now you want to go?"

"I just want to know that when you dream, me and the boy, we're always in your dreams."

He leaned his head on her shoulders and drifted off to

sleep. Her back ached as she sat there with his face pressed against her collar bone. He drooled and the saliva dripped down to her breasts, soaking her frayed polyester bra. She listened to the crickets while watching her son play, muttering his lines to himself as he went in a circle around the field. The moon was glowing above their heads. Winking at them, as Guy liked to say, on its way to brighter shores.

Opening his eyes, Guy asked her, "How do you think a man is judged after he's gone?"

How did he expect her to answer something like that?

"People don't eat riches," she said. "They eat what it can buy."

"What does that mean, Lili? Don't talk to me in parables. Talk to me honestly."

"A man is judged by his deeds," she said. "The boy never goes to bed hungry. For as long as he's been with us, he's always been fed."

Just as if he had heard himself mentioned, the boy came dashing from the other side of the field, crashing in a heap on top of his parents.

"My new lines," he said. "I have forgotten my new lines."

"Is this how you will be the day of this play, son?" Guy asked. "When people give you big responsibilities, you have to try to live up to them."

The boy had relearned his new lines by the time they went to bed.

That night, Guy watched his wife very closely as she undressed for bed.

"I would like to be the one to rub that piece of lemon on your knees tonight," he said.

She handed him the half lemon, then raised her skirt above her knees.

Her body began to tremble as he rubbed his fingers over her skin.

"You know that question I asked you before," he said, "how a man is remembered after he's gone? I know the answer now. I know because I remember my father, who was a very poor struggling man all his life. I remember him as a man that I would never want to be."

· ❧ ·

Lili got up with the break of dawn the next day. The light came up quickly above the trees. Lili greeted some of the market women as they walked together to the public water fountain.

On her way back, the sun had already melted a few gray clouds. She found the boy standing alone in the yard with a terrified expression on his face, the old withered mushrooms uprooted at his feet. He ran up to meet her, nearly knocking her off balance.

"What happened?" she asked. "Have you forgotten your lines?"

The boy was breathing so heavily that his lips could not form a single word.

"What is it?" Lili asked, almost shaking him with anxiety.

"It's Papa," he said finally, raising a stiff finger in the air.

The boy covered his face as his mother looked up at the sky. A rainbow-colored balloon was floating aimlessly above their heads.

"It's Papa," the boy said. "He is in it."

She wanted to look down at her son and tell him that it wasn't his father, but she immediately recognized the spindly arms, in a bright flowered shirt that she had made, gripping the cables.

· ❀ ·

From the field behind the sugar mill a group of workers were watching the balloon floating in the air. Many were clapping and cheering, calling out Guy's name. A few of the women were waving their head rags at the sky, shouting, "Go! Beautiful, go!"

Lili edged her way to the front of the crowd. Everyone was waiting, watching the balloon drift higher up into the clouds.

"He seems to be right over our heads," said the factory foreman, a short slender mulatto with large buckteeth.

Just then, Lili noticed young Assad, his thick black hair sticking to the beads of sweat on his forehead. His face had the crumpled expression of disrupted sleep.

"He's further away than he seems," said young Assad. "I still don't understand. How did he get up there? You need a whole crew to fly these things."

"I don't know," the foreman said. "One of my workers just came in saying there was a man flying above the factory."

"But how the hell did he start it?" Young Assad was perplexed.

"He just did it," the foreman said.

"Look, he's trying to get out!" someone hollered.

A chorus of screams broke out among the workers.

The boy was looking up, trying to see if his father was really trying to jump out of the balloon. Guy was climbing over the side of the basket. Lili pressed her son's face into her skirt.

Within seconds, Guy was in the air hurtling down towards the crowd. Lili held her breath as she watched him fall. He crashed not far from where Lili and the boy were standing, his blood immediately soaking the landing spot.

The balloon kept floating free, drifting on its way to brighter shores. Young Assad rushed towards the body. He dropped to his knees and checked the wrist for a pulse, then dropped the arm back to the ground.

"It's over!" The foreman ordered the workers back to work.

Lili tried to keep her son's head pressed against her skirt as she moved closer to the body. The boy yanked himself away and raced to the edge of the field where his father's body was lying on the grass. He reached the body as young Assad still knelt examining the corpse. Lili rushed after him.

"He is mine," she said to young Assad. "He is my family. He belongs to me."

Young Assad got up and raised his head to search the sky for his aimless balloon, trying to guess where it would land. He took one last glance at Guy's bloody corpse, then raced to his car and sped away.

The foreman and another worker carried a cot and blanket from the factory.

Little Guy was breathing quickly as he looked at his father's body on the ground. While the foreman draped a sheet over Guy's corpse, his son began to recite the lines from his play.

"*A wall of fire is rising and in the ashes, I see the bones of my people. Not only those people whose dark hollow faces I see daily in the fields, but all those souls who have gone ahead to haunt my dreams. At night I relive once more the last caresses from the hand of a loving father, a valiant love, a beloved friend.*"

"Let me look at him one last time," Lili said, pulling back the sheet.

She leaned in very close to get a better look at Guy's face. There was little left of that countenance that she had loved so much. Those lips that curled when he was teasing her. That large flat nose that felt like a feather when rubbed against hers. And those eyes, those night-colored eyes. Though clouded with blood, Guy's eyes were still bulging open. Lili was searching for some kind of sign—a blink, a smile, a wink—something that would remind her of the man that she had married.

"His eyes aren't closed," the foreman said to Lili. "Do you want to close them, or should I?"

The boy continued reciting his lines, his voice rising to a man's grieving roar. He kept his eyes closed, his fists balled at his side as he continued with his newest lines.

"*There is so much sadness in the faces of my people. I have called on their gods, now I call on our gods. I call on our young. I call on our old. I call on our mighty and the weak.*

I call on everyone and anyone so that we shall all let out one piercing cry that we may either live freely or we should die."

"Do you want to close the eyes?" the foreman repeated impatiently.

"No, leave them open," Lili said. "My husband, he likes to look at the sky."

Night Women

· ❋ ❋ ❋ ·

· ❊ ❊ ❊ ·

I cringe from the heat of the night on my face. I feel as bare as open flesh. Tonight I am much older than the twenty-five years that I have lived. The night is the time I dread most in my life. Yet if I am to live, I must depend on it.

Shadows shrink and spread over the lace curtain as my son slips into bed. I watch as he stretches from a little boy into the broom-size of a man, his height mounting the innocent fabric that splits our one-room house into two spaces, two mats, two worlds.

For a brief second, I almost mistake him for the ghost of his father, an old lover who disappeared with the night's shadows a long time ago. My son's bed stays nestled against the corner, far from the peeking jalousies. I watch as he digs furrows in the pillow with his head. He shifts his small body carefully so as not to crease his Sunday clothes. He wraps my long blood-red scarf around his neck, the one I wear myself during the day to tempt my suitors. I let him have it at night, so that he always has something of mine when my face is out of sight.

I watch his shadow resting still on the curtain. My eyes are drawn to him, like the stars peeking through the small holes in the roof that none of my suitors will fix for me, because they like to watch a scrap of the sky while lying on their naked backs on my mat.

A firefly buzzes around the room, finding him and not me. Perhaps it is a mosquito that has learned the gift of lighting itself. He always slaps the mosquitoes dead on his face without even wáking. In the morning, he will have tiny blood spots on his forehead, as though he had spent the whole night kissing a woman with wide-open flesh wounds on her face.

In his sleep he squirms and groans as though he's already discovered that there is pleasure in touching himself. We have never talked about love. What would he need to know? Love is one of those lessons that you grow to learn, the way one learns that one shoe is made to fit a certain foot, lest it cause discomfort.

There are two kinds of women: day women and night women. I am stuck between the day and night in a golden amber bronze. My eyes are the color of dirt, almost copper if I am standing in the sun. I want to wear my matted tresses in braids as soon as I learn to do my whole head without numbing my arms.

Most nights, I hear a slight whisper. My body freezes as I wonder how long it would take for him to cross the curtain and find me.

He says, "Mommy."

I say, *"Darling."*

Somehow in the night, he always calls me in whispers. I hear the buzz of his transistor radio. It is shaped like a can of cola. One of my suitors gave it to him to plug into his ears so he can stay asleep while Mommy *works*.

There is a place in Ville Rose where ghost women ride the crests of waves while brushing the stars out of their hair. There they woo strollers and leave the stars on the path for them. There are nights that I believe that those ghost women are with me. As much as I know that there are women who sit up through the night and undo patches of cloth that they have spent the whole day weaving. These women, they destroy their toil so that they will always have more to do. And as long as there's work, they will not have to lie next to the lifeless soul of a man whose scent still lingers in another woman's bed.

The way my son reacts to my lips stroking his cheeks decides for me if he's asleep. He is like a butterfly fluttering on a rock that stands out naked in the middle of a stream. Sometimes I see in the folds of his eyes a longing for something that's bigger than myself. We are like faraway lovers, lying to one another, under different moons.

When my smallest finger caresses the narrow cleft beneath his nose, sometimes his tongue slips out of his mouth and he licks my fingernail. He moans and turns away, perhaps thinking that this too is a part of the dream.

I whisper my mountain stories in his ear, stories of the ghost women and the stars in their hair. I tell him of the deadly snakes lying at one end of a rainbow and the hat full of gold lying at the other end. I tell him that if I cross a stream of glass-clear hibiscus, I can make myself a goddess. I blow on his long eyelashes to see if he's truly asleep. My fingers coil themselves into visions of birds on his nose. I want him to forget that we live in a place where nothing lasts.

I know that sometimes he wonders why I take such pains-taking care. Why do I draw half-moons on my sweaty forehead and spread crimson powders on the rise of my cheeks. We put on his ruffled Sunday suit and I tell him that we are expecting a sweet angel and where angels tread, the hosts must be as beautiful as floating hibiscus.

In his sleep, his fingers tug his shirt ruffles loose. He licks his lips from the last piece of sugar candy stolen from my purse.

No more, no more, or your teeth will turn black. I have forgotten to make him brush the mint leaves against his teeth. He does not know that one day a woman like his mother may judge him by the whiteness of his teeth.

It doesn't take long before he is snoring softly. I listen for the shy laughter of his most pleasant dreams. Dreams of angels skipping over his head and occasionally resting their pink heels on his nose.

I hear him humming a song. One of the madrigals they still teach children on very hot afternoons in public schools. *Konpè Jako wa p domi?* Brother Jacques, are you asleep?

The hibiscus rustle in the night outside. I sing along to help him sink deeper into his sleep. I apply another layer of the Egyptian rouge to my cheeks. There are some sparkles in the powder, which make it easier for my visitor to find me in the dark.

Emmanuel will come tonight. He is a doctor who likes big buttocks on women, but my small ones will do. He comes on Tuesdays and Saturdays. He arrives bearing flowers as though he's come to court me. Tonight he brings me bougainvillea. It is always a surprise.

"How is your wife?" I ask.

"Not as beautiful as you."

On Mondays and Thursdays, it is an accordion player named Alexandre. He likes to make the sound of the accordion with his mouth in my ear. The rest of the night, he spends with his breadfruit head rocking on my belly button.

Should my son wake up, I have prepared my fabrication. One day, he will grow too old to be told that a wandering man is a mirage and that naked flesh is a dream. I will tell him that his father has come, that an angel brought him back from Heaven for a while.

The stars slowly slip away from the hole in the roof as the doctor sinks deeper and deeper beneath my body. He throbs and pants. I cover his mouth to keep him from screaming. I see his wife's face in the beads of sweat marching down his chin. He leaves with his body soaking from the dew of our flesh. He calls me an avalanche, a waterfall, when he is satisfied.

After he leaves at dawn, I sit outside and smoke a dry tobacco leaf. I watch the piece-worker women march one another to the open market half a day's walk from where they live. I thank the stars that at least I have the days to myself.

When I walk back into the house, I hear the rise and fall of my son's breath. Quickly, I lean my face against his lips to feel the calming heat from his mouth.

"Mommy, have I missed the angels again?" he whispers softly while reaching for my neck.

I slip into the bed next to him and rock him back to sleep.

"Darling, the angels have themselves a lifetime to come to us."

Between the Pool and
the Gardenias

· ❀ ❀ ❀ ·

·❄ ❄ ❄·

She was very pretty. Bright shiny hair and dark brown skin like mahogany cocoa. Her lips were wide and purple, like those African dolls you see in tourist store windows but could never afford to buy.

I thought she was a gift from Heaven when I saw her on the dusty curb, wrapped in a small pink blanket, a few inches away from a sewer as open as a hungry child's yawn. She was like Baby Moses in the Bible stories they read to us at the Baptist Literary Class. Or Baby Jesus, who was born in a barn and died on a cross, with nobody's lips to kiss before he went. She was just like that. Her still round face. Her eyes closed as though she was dreaming of a far other place.

Her hands were bony, and there were veins so close to the surface that it looked like you could rupture her skin if you touched her too hard. She probably belonged to someone, but the street had no one in it. There was no one there to claim her.

At first I was afraid to touch her. Lest I might disturb the early-morning sun rays streaming across her forehead. She might have been some kind of *wanga,* a charm sent to trap me. My enemies were many and crafty. The girls who slept with my husband while I was still grieving over my miscarriages. They might have sent that vision of loveliness to blind me so that I would never find my way back to the place that I yanked out my head when I got on that broken down minibus and left my village months ago.

The child was wearing an embroidered little blue dress with the letters R-O-S-E on a butterfly collar. She looked the way that I had imagined all my little girls would look. The ones my body could never hold. The ones that somehow got suffocated inside me and made my husband wonder if I was killing them on purpose.

I called out all the names I wanted to give them: Eveline, Josephine, Jacqueline, Hermine, Marie Magdalène, Célianne. I could give her all the clothes that I had sewn for them. All these little dresses that went unused.

At night, I could rock her alone in the hush of my room, rest her on my belly, and wish she were inside.

When I had just come to the city, I saw on Madame's television that a lot of poor city women throw out their babies because they can't afford to feed them. Back in Ville Rose you cannot even throw out the bloody clumps that shoot out of your body after your child is born. It is a crime, they say, and your whole family would consider you wicked if you did it. You have to save every piece of flesh and give it a name and bury it near the roots of a tree so that the world won't fall apart around you.

In the city, I hear they throw out whole entire children.

They throw them out anywhere: on doorsteps, in garbage cans, at gas pumps, sidewalks. In the time that I had been in Port-au-Prince, I had never seen such a child until now.

But Rose. My, she was so clean and warm. Like a tiny angel, a little cherub, sleeping after the wind had blown a lullaby into her little ears.

I picked her up and pressed her cheek against mine.

I whispered to her, "Little Rose, my child," as though that name was a secret.

She was like the palatable little dolls we played with as children—mango seeds that we drew faces on and then called by our nicknames. We christened them with prayers and invited all our little boy and girl friends for colas and cassavas and—when we could get them—some nice butter cookies.

Rose didn't stir or cry. She was like something that was thrown aside after she became useless to someone cruel. When I pressed her face against my heart, she smelled like the scented powders in Madame's cabinet, the mixed scent of gardenias and fish that Madame always had on her when she stepped out of her pool.

· ❀ ·

I have always said my mother's prayers at dawn. I welcomed the years that were slowing bringing me closer to her. For no matter how much distance death tried to put between us, my mother would often come to visit me. Sometimes in the short sighs and whispers of somebody else's voice. Sometimes in somebody else's face. Other times in brief moments in my dreams.

There were many nights when I saw some old women leaning over my bed.

"That there is Marie," my mother would say. "She is now the last one of us left."

Mama had to introduce me to them, because they had all died before I was born. There was my great grandmother Eveline who was killed by Dominican soldiers at the Massacre River. My grandmother Défilé who died with a bald head in a prison, because God had given her wings. My godmother Lili who killed herself in old age because her husband had jumped out of a flying balloon and her grown son left her to go to Miami.

We all salute you Mary, Mother of God. Pray for us poor sinners, from now until the hour of our death. Amen.

I always knew they would come back and claim me to do some good for somebody. Maybe I was to do some good for this child.

I carried Rose with me to the outdoor market in Croix Bossale. I swayed her in my arms like she was and had always been mine.

In the city, even people who come from your own village don't know you or care about you. They didn't notice that I had come the day before with no child. Suddenly, I had one, and nobody asked a thing.

· ❀ ·

In the maid's room, at the house in Pétion-Ville, I laid Rose on my mat and rushed to prepare lunch. Monsieur and Madame sat on their terrace and welcomed the coming afternoon by sipping the sweet out of my sour-sop juice.

They liked that I went all the way to the market every day before dawn to get them a taste of the outside country, away from their protected bourgeois life.

"She is probably one of those *manbos*," they say when my back is turned. "She's probably one of those stupid people who think that they have a spell to make themselves invisible and hurt other people. Why can't none of them get a spell to make themselves rich? It's that voodoo nonsense that's holding us Haitians back."

I lay Rose down on the kitchen table as I dried the dishes. I had a sudden desire to explain to her my life.

"You see, young one, I loved that man at one point. He was very nice to me. He made me feel proper. The next thing I know, it's ten years with him. I'm old like a piece of dirty paper people used to wipe their behinds, and he's got ten different babies with ten different women. I just had to run."

I pretended that it was all mine. The terrace with that sight of the private pool and the holiday ships cruising in the distance. The large television system and all those French love songs and *rara* records, with the talking drums and conch shell sounds in them. The bright paintings with white winged horses and snakes as long and wide as lakes. The pool that the sweaty Dominican man cleaned three times a week. I pretended that it belonged to us: him, Rose, and me.

The Dominican and I made love on the grass once, but he never spoke to me again. Rose listened with her eyes closed even though I was telling her things that were much too strong for a child's ears.

I wrapped her around me with my apron as I fried some

plantains for the evening meal. It's so easy to love somebody, I tell you, when there's nothing else around.

Her head fell back like any other infant's. I held out my hand and let her three matted braids tickle the lifelines in my hand.

"I am glad you are not one of those babies that cry all day long," I told her. "All little children should be like you. I am glad that you don't cry and make a lot of noise. You're just a perfect child, aren't you?"

I put her back in my room when Monsieur and Madame came home for their supper. As soon as they went to sleep, I took her out by the pool so we could talk some more.

You don't just join a family not knowing what you're getting into. You have to know some of the history. You have to know that they pray to Erzulie, who loves men like men love her, because she's mulatto and some Haitian men seem to love her kind. You have to look into your looking glass on the day of the dead because you might see faces there that knew you even before you ever came into this world.

I fell asleep rocking her in a chair that wasn't mine. I knew she was real when I woke up the next day and she was still in my arms. She looked the same as she did when I found her. She continued to look like that for three days. After that, I had to bathe her constantly to keep down the smell.

I once had an uncle who bought pigs' intestines in Ville Rose to sell at the market in the city. Rose began to smell like the intestines after they hadn't sold for a few days.

I bathed her more and more often, sometimes three or four times a day in the pool. I used some of Madame's perfume, but it was not helping. I wanted to take her back to the street where I had found her, but I'd already disturbed her rest and had taken on her soul as my own personal responsibility.

I left her in a shack behind the house, where the Dominican kept his tools. Three times a day, I visited her with my hand over my nose. I watched her skin grow moist, cracked, and sunken in some places, then ashy and dry in others. It seemed like she had aged in four days as many years as there were between me and my dead aunts and grandmothers.

I knew I had to act with her because she was attracting flies and I was keeping her spirit from moving on.

I gave her one last bath and slipped on a little yellow dress that I had sewn while praying that one of my little girls would come along further than three months.

I took Rose down to a spot in the sun behind the big house. I dug a hole in the garden among all the gardenias. I wrapped her in the little pink blanket that I had found her in, covering everything but her face. She smelled so bad that I couldn't even bring myself to kiss her without choking on my breath.

I felt a grip on my shoulder as I lowered her into the small hole in the ground. At first I thought it was Monsieur or Madame, and I was real afraid that Madame would be angry with me for having used a whole bottle of her perfume without asking.

Rose slipped and fell out of my hands as my body was forced to turn around.

"What are you doing?" the Dominican asked.

His face was a deep Indian brown but his hands were bleached and wrinkled from the chemicals in the pool. He looked down at the baby lying in the dust. She was already sprinkled with some of the soil that I had dug up.

Edwidge Danticat

"You see, I saw these faces standing over me in my dreams—"

I could have started my explanation in a million of ways.

"Where did you take this child from?" he asked me in his Spanish Creole.

He did not give me a chance to give an answer.

"I go already." I thought I heard a little merengue in the sway of his voice. "I call the gendarmes. They are coming. I smell that rotten flesh. I know you kill the child and keep it with you for evil."

"You acted too soon," I said.

"You kill the child and keep it in your room."

"You know me," I said. "We've been together."

"I don't know you from the fly on a pile of cow manure," he said. "You eat little children who haven't even had time to earn their souls."

He only kept his hands on me because he was afraid that I would run away and escape.

I looked down at Rose. In my mind I saw what I had seen for all my other girls. I imagined her teething, crawling, crying, fussing, and just misbehaving herself.

Over her little corpse, we stood, a country maid and a Spaniard grounds man. I should have asked his name before I offered him my body.

We made a pretty picture standing there. Rose, me, and him. Between the pool and the gardenias, waiting for the law.

The Missing Peace

· ❦ ❦ ❦ ·

We were playing with leaves shaped like butterflies. Raymond limped from the ashes of the old schoolhouse and threw himself on top of a high pile of dirt. The dust rose in clouds around him, clinging to the lapels of his khaki uniform.

"You should see the sunset from here." He grabbed my legs and pulled me down on top of him. The rusty grass brushed against my chin as I slipped out of his grasp.

I got up and tried to run to the other side of the field, but he caught both my legs and yanked me down again.

"Don't you feel like a woman when you are with me?" He tickled my neck. "Don't you feel beautiful?"

He let go of my waist as I turned over and laid flat on my back. The sun was sliding behind the hills, and the glare made the rocks shimmer like chunks of gold.

"I know I can make you feel like a woman," he said, "so why don't you let me?"

"My grandmother says I can have babies."

"Forget your grandmother."

"Would you tell me again how you got your limp?" I asked to distract him.

It was a question he liked to answer, a chance for him to show his bravery.

"If I tell you, will you let me touch your breasts?"

"It is an insult that you are even asking."

"Will you let me do it?"

"You will never know unless you tell me the story."

He closed his eyes as though the details were never any farther than a stage behind his eyelids.

I already knew the story very well.

"I was on guard one night," he said, taking a deep the-atrical breath. "No one told me that there had been a coup in Port-au-Prince. I was still wearing my old régime uniform. My friend Toto from the youth corps says he didn't know if I was old régime or new régime. So he shot a warning at the uniform. Not at me, but at the uniform.

"The shots were coming fast. I was afraid. I forgot the password. Then one of Toto's bullets hit me on my leg and I remembered. I yelled out the password and he stopped shooting."

"Why didn't you take off your uniform?" I asked, laughing.

He ignored the question, letting his hand wander between the buttons of my blouse.

"Do you remember the password?" he asked.

"Yes."

"I don't tell it to just anyone. Lean closer and whisper it in my ear."

I leaned real close and whispered the word in his ear.

"Don't ever forget it if you're in trouble. It could save your life," he said.

"I will remember."

"Tell me again what it is."

I swallowed a gulp of dusty air and said, "Peace."

A round of gunshots rang through the air, signaling that curfew was about to begin.

"I should go back now," I said.

He made no effort to get up, but raised his hand to his lips and blew me a kiss.

"Look after yourself tonight," I said.

"Peace."

· ❧ ·

On the way home, I cut through a line of skeletal houses that had been torched the night of the coup. A lot of the old régime followers died that night. Others fled to the hills or took boats to Miami.

I rushed past a churchyard, where the security officers sometimes buried the bodies of old régime people. The yard was bordered with a chain link fence. But every once in a while, if you looked very closely, you could see a bushy head of hair poking through the ground.

There was a bed of red hibiscus on the footpath behind the yard. Covering my nose, I pulled up a few stems and ran all the way home with them.

· ❧ ·

My grandmother was sitting in the rocking chair in front of our house, making knots in the sisal rope around her waist.

She grabbed the hibiscus from my hand and threw them on the ground.

"How many times must I tell you?" she said. "Those things grow with blood on them." Pulling a leaf from my hair, she slapped me on the shoulder and shoved me inside the house.

"Somebody rented the two rooms in the yellow house," she said, saliva flying out from between her front teeth. "I want you to bring the lady some needles and thread."

My grandmother had fixed up the yellow house very nicely so that many visitors who passed through Ville Rose came to stay in it. Sometimes our boarders were French and American journalists who wanted to take pictures of the churchyard where you could see the bodies.

I rushed out to my grandmother's garden, hoping to catch a glimpse of our new guest. Then I went over to the basin of rainwater in the yard and took off my clothes. My grandmother scrubbed a handful of mint leaves up and down my back as she ran a comb through my hair.

"It's a lady," said my grandmother. "Don't give her a headful of things to worry about. Things you say, thoughts you have, will decide how people treat you."

"Is the lady alone?"

"She is like all those foreign women. She feels she can be alone. And she smokes too." My grandmother giggled. "She smokes just like an old woman when life gets hard."

"She smokes a pipe?"

"Ladies her age don't smoke pipes."

"Cigarettes, then?"

"I don't want you to ask her to let you smoke any."

"Is she a journalist?" I asked.

"That is no concern of mine," my grandmother said.

"Is she intelligent?"

"Intelligence is not only in reading and writing."

"Is she old régime or new régime?"

"She is like us. The only régime she believe in is God's régime. She says she wants to write things down for posterity."

"What did you tell her when she said that?"

"That I already have posterity. I was once a baby and now I am an old woman. That is posterity."

"If she asks me questions, I am going to answer them," I said.

"One day you will stick your hand in a stew that will burn your fingers. I told her to watch her mouth as to how she talks to people. I told her to watch out for vagabonds like Toto and Raymond."

"Never look them in the eye."

"I told her that too," my grandmother said as she discarded the mint leaves.

My whole body felt taut and taint-free. My grandmother's face softened as she noticed the sheen of cleanliness.

"See, you can be a pretty girl," she said, handing me her precious pouch of needles, thimbles, and thread. "You can be a very pretty girl. Just like your mother used to be."

· ❧ ·

A burst of evening air chilled my face as I walked across to the yellow house. I was wearing my only Sunday outfit, a white lace dress that I had worn to my confirmation two years before.

The lady poked her head through the door after my first knock.

"Mademoiselle Gallant?"

"How do you know my name?"

"My grandmother sent me."

She was wearing a pair of *abakos,* American blue jeans.

"It looks as though your grandmother has put you to some inconvenience," she said. Then she led me into the front room, with its oversized mahogany chairs and a desk that my grandmother had bought especially for the journalists to use when they were working there.

"My name is really Emilie," she said in Creole, with a very heavy American accent. "What do people call you?"

"Lamort."

"How did your name come to be 'death'?"

"My mother died while I was being born," I explained. "My grandmother was really mad at me for that."

"They should have given you your mother's name," she said, taking the pouch of needles, thread, and thimbles from me. "That is the way it should have been done."

She walked over to the table in the corner and picked up a pitcher of lemonade that my grandmother made for all her guests when they first arrived.

"Would you like some?" she said, already pouring the lemonade.

"*Oui,* Madame. Please."

She held a small carton box of butter cookies in front of me. I took one, only one, just as my grandmother would have done.

"Are you a journalist?" I asked her.

"Why do you ask that?"

"The people who stay here in this house usually are, journalists."

She lit a cigarette. The smoke breezed in and out of her mouth, just like her own breath.

"I am not a journalist," she said. "I have come here to pay a little visit."

"Who are you visiting?"

"Just people."

"Why don't you stay with the people you are visiting?"

"I didn't want to bother them."

"Are they old régime or new régime?"

"Who?"

"Your people?"

"Why do you ask?"

"Because things you say, thoughts you have, will decide how people treat you."

"It seems to me, *you* are the journalist," she said.

"What do you believe in? Old régime or new régime?"

"Your grandmother told me to say to anyone who is interested, 'The only régime I believe in is God's régime.' I would wager that you are a very good source for the journalists. Do you have any schooling?"

"A little."

Once again, she held the box of cookies in front of me. I took another cookie, but she kept the box there, in the same place. I took yet another cookie, and another, until the whole box was empty.

"Can you read what it says there?" she asked, pointing at a line of red letters.

"I cannot read American," I said. Though many of the journalists who came to stay at the yellow house had tried to teach me, I had not learned.

"It is not American," she said. "They are French cookies. That says *Le Petit Ecolier.*"

I stuffed my mouth in shame.

"Intelligence is not only in reading and writing," I said.

"I did not mean to make you feel ashamed," she said, dropping her cigarette into the half glass of lemonade in her hand. "I want to ask you a question."

"I will answer if I can."

"My mother was old régime," she said. "*She* was a journalist. For a newspaper called *Libète* in Port-au-Prince."

"She came to Ville Rose?"

"Maybe. Or some other town. I don't know. The people who worked with her in Port-au-Prince think she might be in this region. Do you remember any shootings the night of the coup?"

"There were many shootings," I said.

"Did you see any of the bodies?"

"My grandmother and me, we stayed inside."

"Did a woman come to your door? Did anyone ever say that a woman in a purple dress came to their door?"

"No."

"I hear there is a mass burial site," she said. "Do you know it?"

"Yes. I have taken journalists there."

"I would like to go there. Can you take me?"

"Now?"

"Yes."

She pulled some coins from her purse and placed them on the table.

"I have more," she said.

From the back pocket of her jeans, she took out an envelope full of pictures. I ran my fingers over the glossy paper that froze her mother into all kinds of smiling poses: a skinny brown woman with shiny black hair in short spiral curls.

"I have never seen her," I admitted.

"It is possible that she arrived in the evening, and then the coup took place in the middle of the night. Do you know if they found any dead women the day after the coup?"

"There were no bodies," I said. "That is to say no funerals."

· ❖ ·

I heard my grandmother's footsteps even before she reached the door to the yellow house.

"If you tell her that I'm here, I can't go with you," I said.

"Go into the next room and stay there until I come for you."

My grandmother knocked once and then a second time. I rushed to the next room and crouched in a corner.

The plain white sheets that we usually covered the bed with had been replaced by a large piece of purple cloth. On the cement floor were many small pieces of cloth lined up in squares, one next to the other.

"Thank you for sending me the needles," I heard Emilie say to my grandmother. "I thought I had packed some in my suitcase, but I must have forgotten them."

"My old eyes are not what they used to be," my grandmother

said, in the shy humble voice she reserved for prayers and for total strangers. "But if you need some mending, I can do it for you."

"Thank you," said Emilie, "but I can do the mending myself."

"Very well then. Is my granddaughter here?"

"She had to run off," Emilie said.

"Do you know where she went?"

"I don't know. She was dressed for a very fancy affair."

My grandmother was silent for a minute as her knuckles tapped the wood on the front door.

"I will let you rest now," said my grandmother.

"Thank you for the needles," said Emilie.

Emilie bolted the door after my grandmother had left.

"Is there a way we can leave without her seeing you?" She came into the room with a flashlight and her American passport. "You might get a little beating when you go home."

"What are all these small pieces of cloth for?" I asked.

"I am going to sew them onto that purple blanket," she said. "All her life, my mother's wanted to sew some old things together onto that piece of purple cloth."

She raised a piece of white lace above her head. "That's from my mother's wedding dress."

Grabbing a piece of pink terry cloth, she said, "That's an old baby bib."

Tears were beginning to cloud her eyes. She fought them away fast by pushing her head back.

"Purple," she said, "was Mama's favorite color."

"I can ask my grandmother if she saw your mother," I said.

"When I first came, this afternoon," she said, "I showed her the pictures and, like you, she said no."

"We would tell you if we had seen her."

"I want to go to the churchyard," she said. "You say you have already taken other people there."

"I walk by it every day."

"Let's go then."

"Sometimes the yard's guarded at night," I warned her.

"I have an American passport. Maybe that will help."

"The soldiers don't know the difference. Most of them are like me. They would not be able to identify your cookies either."

"How old are you?" she asked.

"Fourteen."

"At your age, you already have a wide reputation. I have a journalist friend who has stayed in this house. He told me you are the only person who would take me to the yard."

I could not think which particular journalist would have given me such a high recommendation; there had been so many.

"Better to be known for good than bad," I said to her.

"I am ready to go," she announced.

"If she is there, will you take her away?"

"Who?"

"Your mother?"

"I have not thought that far."

"And if you see them carrying her, what will you do? She will belong to them and not you."

"They say a girl becomes a woman when she loses her mother," she said. "You, child, were born a woman."

· ❀ ·

We walked through the footpath in my grandmother's garden, toward the main road.

"I have been having these awful dreams," Emilie whispered as she plucked some leaves off my grandmother's pumpkin vines. "I see my mother sinking into a river, and she keeps calling my name."

A round of gunshots echoed in the distance, signals from the night guards who had no other ways of speaking to one another.

We stopped on the side of the road and waited for a while and then continued on our way.

· ❀ ·

The night air blew the smell of rotting flesh to my nose. We circled the churchyard carefully before finding an entrance route. There was a rustle in the yard, like pieces of tin scraping the moist dirt.

"Who is there?"

I thought she stopped breathing when the voice echoed in the night air.

"I am an American journalist," Emilie said in breathless Creole.

She pulled out her passport and raised it toward a blinding flashlight beam. The guard moved the light away from our faces.

It was Raymond's friend, Toto, the one who had shot at him. He was tall and skinny and looked barely sixteen. He was staring at me as though he was possessed by a spirit. In the night, he did not know me.

He took Emilie's passport and flipped through it quickly.

"What are you doing here?" he asked, handing the passport back to her. "It is after curfew."

"The lady was not feeling well," I said. "So she asked me to take her for a walk."

"Didn't you hear the signals?" asked Toto. "The curfew has already started. You would not want to have blood on your nice communion dress."

Two other soldiers passed us on their way to the field. They were dragging the blood-soaked body of a bearded man with an old election slogan written on a T-shirt across his chest: ALONE WE ARE WEAK, TOGETHER WE ARE A FLOOD. The guards were carrying him, feet first, like a breech birth.

Emilie moved toward the body as though she wanted to see it better.

"You see nothing," Toto said, reaching up to turn Emilie's face. Her eyes twitched from Toto's touch on her cheek.

"Under God's sky, you do this to people!" she hollered in a brazen Creole.

Toto laughed loudly.

"We are doing that poor indigent a favor burying him," he said.

Emilie moved forward, trying to follow the guards taking the body into the yard.

"You see nothing," Toto said again, grabbing her face. She raised her arm as if to strike him. He seized her wrist in midair and whisked her hand behind her back.

"You see nothing," he said, his voice hissing between his teeth. "Repeat after me. You see nothing."

"I see nothing," I said in her place. "The lady does not understand."

"I see you," she said in Creole. "How can that be nothing?"

"Peace, let her go," I said.

"You are a coward," she told him.

He lowered his head so he was staring directly into her eyes. He twisted her arm like a wet rag.

"Peace, have mercy on her," I said.

"Let her ask for herself," he said.

She stamped her feet on his boots. He let go of her hand and tapped his rifle on her shoulder. Emilie looked up at him, angry and stunned. He moved back, aiming his rifle at her head, squinting as though he was going to shoot.

"Peace!" I hollered.

My eyes fell on Raymond's as he walked out of the field. I mouthed the word, pleading for help. *Peace. Peace. Peace.*

"They'll go," Raymond said to Toto.

"Then go!" Toto shouted. "Let me watch you go."

"Let's go," I said to Emilie. "My grandmother will be mad at me if I get killed."

Raymond walked behind us as we went back to the road.

"The password has changed," he said. "Stop saying 'peace.'"

By the time I turned around to look at his face, he was already gone.

· ❀ ·

Emilie and I said nothing to each other on the way back. The sound of bullets continued to ring through the night.

"You never look them in the eye," I told her when we got to the yellow house doorstep.

"Is that how you do it?"

I helped her up the steps and into the house.

"I am going to sew these old pieces of cloth onto my mother's blanket tonight," she said.

She took a needle from my grandmother's bundle and began sewing. Her fingers moved quickly as she stitched the pieces together.

"I should go," I said, eyeing the money still on the table.

"Please, stay. I will pay you more if you stay with me until the morning."

"My grandmother will worry."

"What was your mother's name?" she asked.

"Marie Magdalène," I said.

"They should have given you that name instead of the one you got. Was your mother pretty?"

"I don't know. She never took portraits like the ones you have of yours."

"Did you know those men who were in the yard tonight?"

"Yes."

"I didn't fight them because I didn't want to make trouble for you later," she said. "We should write down their names. For posterity."

"We have already had posterity," I said.

"When?"

"We were babies and we grew old."

"You're still young," she said. "You're not old."

"My grandmother is old for me."

"If she is old for you, then doesn't it matter if you get old? You can't say that. You can't just say what she wants for you to say. I didn't get in a fight with them because I did not want them to hurt you," she said.

"I will stay with you," I said, "because I know you are afraid."

I curled my body on the floor next to her and went to sleep.

· ❀ ·

She had the patches sewn together on the purple blanket when I woke up that morning. On the floor, scattered around her, were the pictures of her mother.

"I became a woman last night," she said. "I lost my mother and all my other dreams."

Her voice was weighed down with pain and fatigue. She picked up the coins from the table, added a dollar from her purse, and pressed the money into my palm.

"Will you whisper their names in my ear?" she asked. "I will write them down."

"There is Toto," I said. "He is the one that hit you."

"And the one who followed us?"

"That is Raymond who loves leaves shaped like butterflies."

She jotted their names on the back of one of her mother's pictures and gave it to me.

"My mother's name was Isabelle," she said. "Keep this for posterity."

· ❀ ·

Outside, the morning sun was coming out to meet the day. Emilie sat on the porch and watched me go to my grandmother's house. Loosely sewn, the pieces on the purple blanket around her shoulders were coming apart.

My grandmother was sitting in front of the house waiting for me. She did not move when she saw me. Nor did she make a sound.

"Today, I want you to call me by another name," I said.

"Haughty girls don't get far," she said, rising from the chair.

"I want you to call me by her name," I said.

She looked pained as she watched me moving closer to her.

"Marie Magdalène?"

"Yes, Marie Magdalène," I said. "I want you to call me Marie Magdalène." I liked the sound of that.

Seeing Things Simply

· ❧ ❧ ❧ ·

· ❧ ❧ ❧ ·

"Get it! Kill it!"

The cock fight had just begun. Princesse heard the shouting from the school yard as she came out of class. The rooster that crowed the loudest usually received the first blow. It was often the first to die.

The cheers burst into a roar. As Princesse crossed the dusty road, she could hear the men shouting. "Take its head off! Go for its throat!"

At night, *vodou* ceremonies were held around the shady banyan tree that rose from the middle of an open hut. However, during the days the villagers held animal fights there, and sometimes even weddings and funerals. Outside the fight ring, a few women sold iced drinks and tickets to the Dominican lottery.

There was an old man in front of the yard smoking a badly carved wooden pipe.

"Let's go home," his wife was saying to him as she balanced a heavy basket on her head.

"Let me be or I'll make you hush," he shouted at her.

He dug his foot deep into the brown dusty grass to put a spell on her that would make her mute.

The wife threw her head back all the way, so far that you could have cut her throat and she wouldn't have felt it. She laughed like she was chortling at the clouds and walked away.

The man blew his pipe smoke in his wife's direction. He continued to push his foot deep into the grass, cursing his wife as she went on her way, the basket swaying from side to side on her head.

"What a pretty girl you are." The old man winked as Princesse approached him. The closer Princesse came, the more clearly she could see his face. He was a former schoolteacher from the capital who had moved to Ville Rose, as far as anyone could tell, to get drunk.

The old man was handsome in an odd kind of way, with a gray streak running through the middle of his hair. He sat outside of the cockfights every day, listening as though it were a kind of music, shooing away his wife with spells that never worked.

There was talk in the village that he was a very educated man, had studied at the Sorbonne in Paris, France. The word was that such a man would only live with a woman who carried a basket on her head because he himself had taken a big fall in the world. He might be running from the law, or maybe a charm had been placed on him, which would explain why every ordinary hex he tried to put on his wife failed to work.

"How are you today?" he asked, reaching for the hem of Princesse's dress. Princesse was sixteen but because she was very short and thin could easily pass for twelve. "Do you want to place a wager on the roosters?" he asked her jokingly.

"No sir," she said as she continued on her way.

The old man took a gulp from a bottle filled with rum and leaves and limped towards the yard where the fight was taking place.

The roosters were whimpering. The battle was near its end. There was another loud burst of cheers, this one longer than the last. It was the sound of a cheerful death. One of the roosters had lost the fight.

· ❧ ·

Princesse was on her way to keep an appointment with Catherine, a painter from Guadeloupe. A row of houses in Ville Rose was occupied by a group of foreigners. Princesse had met a few of them through the teachers at her school. The students in her class were rewarded for good grades by being introduced to the French-speaking artists and writers who lived in the gingerbread houses perched on the hills that overlooked Ville Rose's white sand beaches.

Catherine was reading on the beach when Princesse called down to her from the hill.

"Madame," Princesse said, calling upon her phonetics lessons in order to sound less native and more French.

Catherine put down her book and threw a thigh-length robe over her bathing suit as she ran up to the house. There, she kissed Princesse on both cheeks as though they were meeting at a party.

Catherine was only twenty-seven years old but looked

much older. She sunbathed endlessly, but her skin stayed the same copper-tinged shade, even as it became more and more dried out. Of any black person that Princesse knew, Catherine spent the most time in the sun without changing color.

Catherine already had her canvas and paint set up on the veranda of her house. She liked to paint outdoors in the sun.

"Relax, *chérie,*" she assured Princesse. "Just take your own time to become comfortable. Heaven and earth will be here long after we're gone. We're in no rush."

Princesse slowly removed the checkered blouse of her school uniform, followed by a spotless white undershirt she wore to keep her blouse from getting stained with sweat. She had breasts like mushrooms, big ones that just hadn't spread yet.

Catherine began to sketch as Princesse took off her skirt. It was always hardest getting Princesse to remove her panties, but once Catherine either turned around or pretended to close her eyes, they were gone in a flash.

"Now we work," Catherine said to Princesse as the girl reclined on a white sheet that Catherine had laid out for her on the floor of the veranda. Princesse liked to sit beneath the rail of the veranda, hidden from the view of any passersby.

One day Catherine hoped to get Princesse to roam naked on the beach attempting to make love to the crest of an ocean wave, but for now it was enough for her to make Princesse comfortable with her nudity while safely hidden from the sight of onlookers.

"It's not so bad," Catherine said, making quick pencil

strokes on the sketch pad in her hand to delineate Princesse's naked breasts. "Relax. Pretend that you're in your bed alone and very comfortable."

It was hard for Princesse to pretend with ease as the sun beamed into her private parts.

"Remember what I've told you," Catherine said. "I will never use your name and no one who lives in this village will ever see these paintings."

Princesse relaxed in the glow of this promise.

"One day your grandchildren will walk into galleries in France," Catherine said, "and *there* they'll admire your beautiful body."

There was nothing so beautiful about her body, Princesse thought. She had a body like all the others who lived here except she was willing to be naked. But after she was dead and buried, she wouldn't care who saw her body. It would be up to Catherine and God to decide that. As long as Catherine never showed anyone in Ville Rose the portraits, she would be content.

Catherine never displayed any intention of sharing her work with Princesse. After she felt that she had painted enough of them, Catherine would pack up her canvases and bring them to either Paris or to Guadeloupe for safekeeping.

Catherine stopped sketching for a second to get herself a glass of iced rum. She offered some to Princesse, who shook her head, no. The village would surely smell the rum on her breath when she returned home and would conjecture quickly as to where she had gotten it.

"I used to pose for classes when I was in France." Catherine leaned back on the rail of the veranda and slowly sipped.

"I posed for art students in Paris. That's how I made my living for a while."

"How was it?" Princesse asked, her eyes closed against the glare of the sun as it bounced off the glass of clear white rum in Catherine's hand.

"It was very difficult for me," Catherine answered, "just as it is for you. The human form in all its complexity is not the easiest thing to re-create. It is hard to catch a likeness of a person unless the artist knows the person very well. That's why, once you find someone whose likeness you've mastered, it's hard to let them go."

Catherine picked up the pad once more. Princesse lay back and said nothing. A wandering fly parked itself on her nose. She smacked it away. A streak of coconut pomade melting in Princesse's hair fell onto the white sheet stretched out on the veranda floor beneath her. The grease made a stain on the mat like the spots her period often made in the back of her dresses.

"No two faces are ever the same," Catherine said, her wrist moving quickly back and forth across the pad. The pencil made a slight sweeping noise as though it were grating down the finer, more resistant surfaces of the white page. "The eyes are the most striking and astonishing aspects of the face."

"What about the mouth?" Princesse asked.

"That is very crucial too, my dear, because the lips determine the expression of the face."

Princesse pulled her lips together in an exaggerated pout.

"You mean like that?" she asked, giggling.

"Exactly," Catherine said.

· ❖ ·

Catherine flipped the cover of her pad when she was done.

"You can go now, Princesse," she said.

Princesse dressed quickly. Catherine squeezed two gourdes between her palms, kissing her twice on the cheek.

Princesse rushed down the steps leading away from the beach house. She kept walking until she reached the hard dirt road that stretched back to the village.

· ❖ ·

It was nightfall. In a cloud of dust, an old jeep clattered down the road.

Someone was playing a drum in the fight yard. The calls of conch shells and hollow cow horns were attempting to catch up to the insistent rhythm.

A man wept as he buried his rooster, which had died in one of the fights that afternoon. "Ayïbobo," the man said, chanting to the stars as he dropped the bird into a small hole that he had dug along the side of the road. One of the stars answered by plunging down from the sky, landing in a fiery ball behind a hill.

"You could have eaten that rooster!" the old drunk hollered at him. "I'm going to come and get that bird tonight and eat it with my wife on Sunday. What a waste!"

"I am giving it back to my father!" hollered back the distressed man. "He gave me this bird last year."

"Your father is dead, you fool!" cried the old drunk.

"I am giving this bird back to him."

The old man was still sitting by the fence cradling his leaf-crammed bottle of rum.

"My great luck, twice in a day, I get to see you," he said to Princesse as she walked by.

"Twice in a day," Princesse agreed, the wind blowing through her skirt.

The human body is an extremely complex form. So Princesse was learning. A good painting would not only capture the old man's features but also his moods and personality. This could be done with a lot of fancy brush strokes or with one single flirting line, all depending on the skill of the artist. Each time she went to Catherine's, Princesse would learn something different.

· ❖ ·

The next day, Catherine had her sit fully clothed on a rock on the beach as she painted her on canvas. Princesse watched her own skin grow visibly darker as she sat near the open sea, the waves spraying a foam of white sand onto her toes.

"In the beginning God said, 'Let there be light.'" Catherine's brush attacked the canvas as she spoke, quickly mixing burnished colors to catch the harsh afternoon light. "Without light, there is nothing. We might as well be blind people. No light or colors."

For the moment, Catherine was painting the rock and the sand beneath Princesse, ignoring the main subject. She was waiting for just the right moment to add Princesse to the canvas. She might even do it later, after the sun had set, when she could paint at her leisure. She might do it the next day when the light would have changed slightly, when the sun was just a little higher or lower in the sky, turning the sea a different shade.

"It's dazzling how the light filters through your complexion," Catherine assured Princesse. "They say black absorbs all color. It blots and consumes it and gives us nothing back. That's wrong, don't you think?"

"Of course," Princesse nodded. Catherine was the expert. She was always right.

"Black skin gives so much to the canvas," Catherine continued. "Do you ever think of how we change things and how they change us?"

"How?" ventured Princesse.

"Perhaps the smaller things—like human beings, for example—can also change and affect the bigger things in the universe."

· ❖ ·

A few days later, Princesse sat in Catherine's bedroom as Catherine sketched her seated in a rocking chair holding a tall red candle in each hand. Black drapes on the window kept out the light of the afternoon sky. A small mole of melted candle wax grew on Princesse's hand as she sat posing stiffly.

"When I was just beginning to paint in Paris," Catherine told Princesse in the dark, "I used to live with a man who was already an artist. He told me that if I wanted to be an artist, I would have to wear boots, a pair of his large clunky boots with holes in the soles. That man was my best teacher. He died yesterday."

"I am sorry," Princesse said, seeing no real strain of loss in Catherine's eyes.

"It's fine," Catherine said. "He was old and sickly."

"What was it like, wearing those shoes?" Princesse asked.

"I see where your interests lie," Catherine said.

"I am sorry if that was insensitive."

"I would tell him to go somewhere and perform obscene acts on himself every time he told me to wear the boots," Catherine said, "but whenever he went on a trip, I would make myself live in those shoes. I wore them every day, everywhere I went. I would wear them on the street, in the park, to the butcher's. I wore them everywhere I could until they felt like mine for a while."

· ❁ ·

The next day when Princesse went to see Catherine, she did not paint her. Instead they sat on the veranda while Catherine drank white rum.

"Let me hear you talk," Catherine said. "Tell me, what color do you think the sky is right now?"

Princesse looked up and saw a color typical of the Haitian sky.

"I guess it's blue," Princesse said. "Indigo, maybe, like the kind we use in the wash."

"We have so much here," Catherine said. "Even wash indigo in the sky."

· ❁ ·

Catherine was not home when Princesse came the next afternoon. Princesse waited outside on the beach-house steps until it was almost nightfall. Finally, Princesse walked down to the beach and watched the stars line up in random battalions in the evening sky.

There was a point in the far distance where the sky almost seemed to blend with the sea, stroking the surface the way two people's lips would touch each other's.

Standing there, Princesse wished she could paint that. That and all the night skies that she had seen, the full moon and the stars peeking down like tiny gods acting out their will, plunging and sometimes winking in a tease, in a parade ignored by humankind. Princesse thought that she could paint that, giving it light and color, shape and texture, all those things that Catherine spoke of.

· ❖ ·

Princesse returned the following day to find Catherine still absent. She walked the perimeter of the deserted house at least three dozen times until her ankles ached. Again Princesse stayed until the evening to watch the sky over the beach. As she walked along, she picked up a small conch shell and began to blow a song into it.

Princesse wanted to paint the sound that came out of the shell, a moan like a call to a distant ship, an SOS with a dissonant melody. She wanted to paint the feel of the sand beneath her toes, the crackling of dry empty crab shells as she popped them between her palms. She wanted to paint herself, but taller and more curvaceous, with a stream of silky black mermaid's hair. She wanted to discover where the sky and the sea meet each other like two old paramours who had been separated for a very long time.

Princesse carried the conch shell in her hand as she strolled. She dug the sharp tip of the shell into her index finger and drew a few drops of blood. The blood dripped onto the front of her white undershirt, making small blots that sank into the cloth, leaving uneven circles. Princesse sat on the cooling sand on the beach staring at the spots on her otherwise immaculate undershirt, seeing in the blank space all kinds of possibilities.

· ❋ ·

Catherine came back a week later. Princesse returned to the beach and found her stretched out in a black robe, in her usual lounging chair, reading a magazine.

"Madame," Princesse called from the road, rushing eagerly towards Catherine.

"I am sorry," Catherine said. "I had to go to Paris."

Catherine folded the magazine and started walking back to the house.

As Princesse had expected, all the painted canvases were gone. Catherine offered her some iced rum on the veranda. This time Princesse gladly accepted. She would chew some mint leaves before going home.

Catherine did not notice the blood stains on the undershirt that Princesse had worn every day since she'd drawn on it with her own blood. Catherine sifted through a portfolio of recent work and pulled out a small painting of

Princesse lying naked on the beach rock with a candle in each hand.

"I had a burst of creativity when I was in Paris," she said. "Here, it's yours."

Princesse peered at this re-creation, not immediately recognizing herself, but then seeing in the face, the eyes, the breasts, a very true replication of her body.

Princesse stared at the painting for a long time and then she picked it up, cradling it as though it were a child. It was the first time that Catherine had given *her* one of her paintings. Princesse felt like she had helped to give birth to something that would have never existed otherwise.

"My friend, the artist whose boots I used to wear," Catherine said, "I wanted to go to Paris if only to see his grave. I missed the funeral, but I wanted to see where his bones were resting."

Catherine gave Princesse two T-shirts, one from the Pompidou Center, and another from a museum in Paris where she hoped one day her work would hang.

"I wish I could have let you know I was going," Catherine said. "But I wasn't sure myself that I would go until I got on the plane."

Princesse sat on the veranda next to Catherine, holding her little painting. She was slowly becoming familiar with what she saw there. It was her all right, recreated.

It struck Princesse that this is why she wanted to make pictures, to have something to leave behind even after she was gone, something that showed what she had observed in a way that no one else had and no one else would after her. The sky in all its glory had been there for eons even before she came into the world, and there it would stay with its crashing stars and moody clouds. The sand and its caresses, the conch and its melody would be there forever as well. All that would change would be the faces of the people who would see and touch those things, faces like hers, which was already not as it had been a few years before and which would mature and change in the years to come.

· ❧ ·

That afternoon, as Princesse walked up the road near the cockfights, clutching an image of herself frozen in a time that would never repeat, a man walked out of the yard, carrying a fiery red rooster with a black sock draped over its face. The rooster was still and lifeless beneath the sock even as the man took sips of white rum and blew it in a cloud at the rooster's shrouded head. A few drops of blood fell to the earth in a circle and vanished in the dirt.

Along the fence, the old drunk was moaning a melody that Princesse had never heard him sing before, a sad longing tune that reminded her of the wail of the conch shell.

"I am a lucky man, twice a day I see you," he said.

"Twice a day," she replied.

The old man dug his heel into the dust as his wife approached him, trying to take him home.

Princesse watched the couple from a safe distance, cradling her portrait in her arms. When she was far enough away not to be noticed, she sat on a patch of grass under a tree and began to draw their two faces in the dust. First she drew a silhouette of the old man and then his wife with her basket on her head, perched over him like a ballerina, unaware of her load.

When she was done, Princesse got up and walked away, leaving the blank faces in the dirt for the next curious voyeur to add a stroke to.

In the yard nearby another cockfight had begun.

"Get him, kill him!" the men cheered. "Take his head off. Right now!"

New York Day Women

· ❈ ❈ ❈ ·

·❧ ❧ ❧·

Today, walking down the street, I see my mother. She is strolling with a happy gait, her body thrust toward the don't walk sign and the yellow taxicabs that make forty-five-degree turns on the corner of Madison and Fifty-seventh Street.

I have never seen her in this kind of neighborhood, peering into Chanel and Tiffany's and gawking at the jewels glowing in the Bulgari windows. My mother never shops outside of Brooklyn. She has never seen the advertising office where I work. She is afraid to take the subway, where you may meet those young black militant street preachers who curse black women for straightening their hair.

Yet, here she is, my mother, who I left at home that morning in her bathrobe, with pieces of newspapers twisted like rollers in her hair. My mother, who accuses me of random offenses as I dash out of the house.

·❧·

Would you get up and give an old lady like me your subway seat? In this state of mind, I bet you don't even give up your seat to a pregnant lady.

· ❧ ·

My mother, who is often right about that. Sometimes I get up and give my seat. Other times, I don't. It all depends on how pregnant the woman is and whether or not she is with her boyfriend or husband and whether or not *he* is sitting down.

As my mother stands in front of Carnegie Hall, one taxi driver yells to another, "What do you think this is, a dance floor?"

My mother waits patiently for this dispute to be settled before crossing the street.

· ❧ ·

In Haiti when you get hit by a car, the owner of the car gets out and kicks you for getting blood on his bumper.

· ❧ ·

My mother who laughs when she says this and shows a large gap in her mouth where she lost three more molars to the dentist last week. My mother, who at fifty-nine, says dentures are okay.

· ❧ ·

You can take them out when they bother you. I'll like them.
I'll like them fine.

· ❀ ·

Will it feel empty when Papa kisses you?

· ❀ ·

Oh no, he doesn't kiss me that way anymore.

· ❀ ·

My mother, who watches the lottery drawing every night on
channel 11 without ever having played the numbers.

· ❀ ·

**A third of that money is all I would need. We would pay the
mortgage, and your father could stop driving that taxicab all
over Brooklyn.**

· ❀ ·

I follow my mother, mesmerized by the many possibilities of her journey. Even in a flowered dress, she is lost in a sea
of pinstripes and gray suits, high heels and elegant short
skirts, Reebok sneakers, dashing from building to building.
My mother, who won't go out to dinner with anyone.

· ❧ ·

If they want to eat with me, let them come to my house, even if I boil water and give it to them.

· ❧ ·

My mother, who talks to herself when she peels the skin off poultry.

· ❧ ·

Fat, you know, and cholesterol. Fat and cholesterol killed your aunt Hermine.

· ❧ ·

My mother, who makes jam with dried grapefruit peel and then puts in cinnamon bark that I always think is cockroaches in the jam. My mother, whom I have always bought household appliances for, on her birthday. A nice rice cooker, a blender.

I trail the red orchids in her dress and the heavy faux leather bag on her shoulders. Realizing the ferocious pace of my pursuit, I stop against a wall to rest. My mother keeps on walking as though she owns the sidewalk under her feet.

As she heads toward the Plaza Hotel, a bicycle messenger swings so close to her that I want to dash forward and rescue her, but she stands dead in her tracks and lets him ride around her and then goes on.

My mother stops at a corner hot-dog stand and asks for

something. The vendor hands her a can of soda that she slips into her bag. She stops by another vendor selling sundresses for seven dollars each. I can tell that she is looking at an African print dress, contemplating my size. I think to myself, Please Ma, don't buy it. It would be just another thing that I would bury in the garage or give to Goodwill.

· ❀ ·

Why should we give to Goodwill when there are so many people back home who need clothes? We save our clothes for the relatives in Haiti.

· ❀ ·

Twenty years we have been saving all kinds of things for the relatives in Haiti. I need the place in the garage for an exercise bike.

· ❀ ·

You are pretty enough to be a stewardess. Only dogs like bones.

· ❀ ·

This mother of mine, she stops at another hot-dog vendor's and buys a frankfurter that she eats on the street. I never knew that she ate frankfurters. With her blood pressure, she shouldn't eat anything with sodium. She has to be careful with her heart, this day woman.

· ❁ ·

I cannot just swallow salt. Salt is heavier than a hundred bags of shame.

· ❁ ·

She is slowing her pace, and now I am too close. If she turns around, she might see me. I let her walk into the park before I start to follow again.

My mother walks toward the sandbox in the middle of the park. There a woman is waiting with a child. The woman is wearing a leotard with biker's shorts and has small weights in her hands. The woman kisses the child good-bye and surrenders him to my mother; then she bolts off, running on the cemented stretches in the park.

The child given to my mother has frizzy blond hair. His hand slips into hers easily, like he's known her for a long time. When he raises his face to look at my mother, it is as though he is looking at the sky.

My mother gives this child the soda that she bought from the vendor on the street corner. The child's face lights up as she puts in a straw in the can for him. This seems to be a conspiracy just between the two of them.

My mother and the child sit and watch the other children play in the sandbox. The child pulls out a comic book from a knapsack with Big Bird on the back. My mother peers into his comic book. My mother, who taught herself to read as a little girl in Haiti from the books that her brothers brought home from school.

My mother, who has now lost six of her seven sisters in Ville Rose and has never had the strength to return for their funerals.

· ❧ ·

Many graves to kiss when I go back. Many graves to kiss.

· ❧ ·

She throws away the empty soda can when the child is done with it. I wait and watch from a corner until the woman in the leotard and biker's shorts returns, sweaty and breathless, an hour later. My mother gives the woman back her child and strolls farther into the park.

I turn around and start to walk out of the park before my mother can see me. My lunch hour is long since gone. I have to hurry back to work. I walk through a cluster of joggers, then race to a *Sweden Tours* bus. I stand behind the bus and take a peek at my mother in the park. She is standing in a circle, chatting with a group of women who are taking other people's children on an afternoon outing. They look like a Third World Parent-Teacher Association meeting.

I quickly jump into a cab heading back to the office. Would Ma have said hello had she been the one to see me first?

As the cab races away from the park, it occurs to me that perhaps one day I would chase an old woman down a street by mistake and that old woman would be somebody else's mother, who I would have mistaken for mine.

· ❀ ·

Day women come out when nobody expects them.

· ❀ ·

Tonight on the subway, I will get up and give my seat to a pregnant woman or a lady about Ma's age.

My mother, who stuffs thimbles in her mouth and then blows up her cheeks like Dizzy Gillespie while sewing yet another Raggedy Ann doll that she names Suzette after me.

· ❀ ·

I will have all these little Suzettes in case you never have any babies, which looks more and more like it is going to happen.

· ❀ ·

My mother who had me when she was thirty-three—*l'âge du Christ*—at the age that Christ died on the cross.

· ❀ ·

That's a blessing, believe you me, even if American doctors say by that time you can make retarded babies.

· ❀ ·

My mother, who sews lace collars on my company softball T-shirts when she does my laundry.

· ❧ ·

Why, you can't you look like a lady playing softball?

· ❧ ·

My mother, who never went to any of my Parent-Teacher Association meetings when I was in school.

· ❧ ·

You're so good anyway. What are they going to tell me? I don't want to make you ashamed of this day woman. Shame is heavier than a hundred bags of salt.

Caroline's Wedding

❀ ❀ ❀

· ❧ ❧ ❧ ·

It was a cool September day when I walked out of a Brooklyn courtroom holding my naturalization certificate. As I stood on the courthouse steps, I wanted to run back to my mother's house waving the paper like the head of an enemy rightfully conquered in battle.

I stopped at the McDonald's in Fulton Mall to call ahead and share the news.

There was a soap opera playing in the background when she picked up the phone.

"I am a citizen, Ma," I said.

I heard her clapping, the way she had applauded our good deeds when Caroline and I were little girls.

"The paper they gave me, it looks nice," I said. "It's wide like a diploma and has a gold seal with an official-looking signature at the bottom. Maybe I will frame it."

"The passport, weren't you going to bring it to the post office to get a passport right away?" she asked in Creole.

"But I want you to see it, Ma."

"Go ahead and get the passport. I can see it when you get it back," she said. "A passport is truly what's American. May it serve you well."

At the post office on Flatbush Avenue, I had to temporarily trade in my naturalization certificate for a passport application. Without the certificate, I suddenly felt like unclaimed property. When my mother was three months pregnant with my younger sister, Caroline, she was arrested in a sweatshop raid and spent three days in an immigration jail. In my family, we have always been very anxious about our papers.

· ❧ ·

I raced down the block from where the number eight bus dropped me off, around the corner from our house. The fall was slowly settling into the trees on our block, some of them had already turned slightly brown.

I could barely contain my excitement as I walked up the steps to the house, sprinting across the living room to the kitchen.

Ma was leaning over the stove, the pots clanking as she hummed a song to herself.

"My passport should come in a month or so," I said, unfolding a photocopy of the application for her to see.

She looked at it as though it contained boundless possibilities.

"We can celebrate with some strong bone soup," she said. "I am making some right now."

In the pot on the stove were scraps of cow bones stewing in hot bubbling broth.

Ma believed that her bone soup could cure all kinds of ills.

She even hoped that it would perform the miracle of detaching Caroline from Eric, her Bahamian fiancé. Since Caroline had announced that she was engaged, we'd had bone soup with our supper every single night.

"Have you had some soup?" I asked, teasing Caroline when she came out of the bedroom.

"This soup is really getting on my nerves," Caroline whispered in my ear as she walked by the stove to get some water from the kitchen faucet.

Caroline had been born without her left forearm. The round end of her stub felt like a stuffed dumpling as I squeezed it hello. After my mother was arrested in the sweatshop immigration raid, a prison doctor had given her a shot of a drug to keep her calm overnight. That shot, my mother believed, caused Caroline's condition. Caroline was lucky to have come out missing only one forearm. She might not have been born at all.

"Soup is ready," Ma announced.

"If she keeps making this soup," Caroline whispered, "I will dip my head into the pot and scald myself blind. That will show her that there's no magic in it."

It was very hard for Ma to watch Caroline prepare to leave us, knowing that there was nothing she could do but feed her.

"Ma, if we keep on with this soup," Caroline said, "we'll all grow horns like the ones that used to be on these cows."

Caroline brushed aside a strand of her hair, chemically straightened and streaked bright copper from a peroxide experiment.

"You think you are so American," Ma said to Caroline.

"You don't know what's good for you. You have no taste buds. A double tragedy."

"There's another American citizen in the family now." I took advantage of the moment to tell Caroline.

"Congratulations," she said. "I don't love you any less."

Caroline had been born in America, something that she very much took for granted.

· ❀ ·

Later that night, Ma called me into her bedroom after she thought Caroline had gone to sleep. The room was still decorated just the way it had been when Papa was still alive. There was a large bed, almost four feet tall, facing an old reddish brown dresser where we could see our reflections in a mirror as we talked.

Ma's bedroom closet was spilling over with old suitcases, some of which she had brought with her when she left Haiti almost twenty-five years before. They were so crowded into the small space that the closet door would never stay fully closed.

"She drank all her soup," Ma said as she undressed for bed. "She talks bad about the soup but she drinks it."

"Caroline is not a child, Ma."

"She doesn't have to drink it."

"She wants to make you happy in any small way she can."

"If she wanted to make me happy, you know what she would do."

"She has the right to choose who she wants to marry. That's none of our business."

"I am afraid she will never find a nice man to marry her," Ma said. "I am afraid you won't either."

"Caroline is already marrying a nice man," I said.

"She will never find someone Haitian," she said.

"It's not the end of creation that she's not marrying someone Haitian."

"No one in our family has ever married outside," she said. "There has to be a cause for everything."

"What's the cause of you having said what you just said? You know about Eric. You can't try to pretend that he's not there."

"She is my last child. There is still a piece of her inside me."

"Why don't you give her a spanking?" I joked.

"My mother used to spank me when I was older than you," she said. "Do you know how your father came to have me as his wife? *His* father wrote a letter to my father and came to my house on a Sunday afternoon and brought the letter in a pink and green handkerchief. Pink because it is the color of romance and green for hope that it might work. Your grandfather on your papa's side had the handkerchief sewn especially in these two colors to wrap my proposal letter in. He brought this letter to my house and handed it to my father. My father didn't even read the letter himself. He called in a neighbor and asked the neighbor to read it out loud.

"The letter said in very fancy words how much your father wanted to be my husband. *My son desires greatly your daughter's hand,* something like that. The whole time the letter was being read, your father and I sat silently while our parents had this type of show. Then my father sent your father away, saying that he and my mother wanted to think about the proposal."

"Did they consult you about it?" I asked, pretending not to know the outcome.

"Of course they did. I had to act like I didn't really like your father or that at least I liked him just a tiny little bit. My parents asked me if I wanted to marry him and I said I wouldn't mind, but they could tell from my face that it was a different story, that I was already desperately in love."

"But you and Papa had talked about this, right? Before his father came to your father."

"Your father and I had talked about it. We were what you girls call dating. He would come to my house and I would go to his house when his mother was there. We would go to the cinema together, but the proposal, it was all very formal, and sometimes, in some circumstances, formality is important."

"What would you have done if your father had said no?" I asked.

"Don't say that you will never dine with the devil if you have a daughter," she said. "You never know what she will bring. My mother and father, they knew that too."

"What would you have done if your father had said no?" I repeated.

"I probably would have married anyway," she said. "There is little others can do to keep us from our hearts' desires."

Caroline too was going to get married whether Ma wanted her to or not. That night, maybe for the first time, I saw a hint of this realization in Ma's face. As she raised her comforter and slipped under the sheets, she looked as if she were all alone in the world, as lonely as a woman with two grown daughters could be.

"We're not like birds," she said, her head sinking into the pillow. "We don't just kick our children out of our nests."

· ❧ ·

Caroline was still awake when I returned to our room.

"Is she ever going to get tired of telling that story?" she asked.

"You're talking about a woman who has had soup with cow bones in it for all sixty years of her life. She doesn't get tired of things. What are you going to do about it?"

"She'll come around. She has to," Caroline said.

We sat facing each other in the dark, playing a free-association game that Ma had taught us when we were girls.

"Who are you?" Caroline asked me.

"I am the *lost* child of the night."

"Where do you come from?"

"I come from the inside of the *lost* stone."

"Where are your eyes?"

"I have eyes *lost* behind my head, where they can best protect me."

"Who is your mother?"

"She who is the *lost* mother of all."

"Who is your father?"

"He who is the *lost* father of all."

Sometimes we would play half the night, coming up with endless possibilities for questions and answers, only repeating the key word in every sentence. Ma too had learned this game when she was a girl. Her mother belonged to a secret women's society in Ville Rose, where the women had to question each other before entering one another's houses. Many nights while her mother was hosting the late-night meetings, Ma would fall asleep listening to the women's voices.

"I just remembered. There is a Mass Sunday at Saint Agnes for a dead refugee woman." Ma was standing in the doorway in her nightgown. "Maybe you two will come with me."

"Nobody sleeps in this house," Caroline said.

I would go, but not her.

· ❊ ·

They all tend to be similar, farewell ceremonies to the dead. The church was nearly empty, with a few middle-aged women scattered in the pews.

I crossed myself as I faced the wooden life-size statue of a dying Christ, looking down on us from high above the altar. The chapel was dim except for a few high chandeliers and the permanent glow of the rich hues of the stained glass windows. Ma kneeled in one of the side pews. She clutched her rosary and recited her Hail Marys with her eyes tightly shut.

For a long time, services at Saint Agnes have been tailored to fit the needs of the Haitian community. A line of altar boys proceeded down the aisle, each carrying a long lit candle. Ma watched them as though she were a spectator at a parade. Behind us, a group of women was carrying on a conversation, criticizing a neighbor's wife who, upon leaving Haiti, had turned from a sweet Haitian wife into a self-willed tyrant.

"In New York, women give their eight hours to the white

man," one of the worshipers said in the poor woman's defense. "No one has time to be cradling no other man."

There was a slow drumbeat playing like a death march from the altar. A priest in a black robe entered behind the last altar boy. He walked up to the altar and began to read from a small book.

Ma lowered her head so far down that I could see the dip in the back of her neck, where she had a port-wine mark shaped like Manhattan Island.

"We have come here this far, from the shackles of the old Africans," read the priest in Creole. "At the mercy of the winds, at the mercy of the sea, to the quarters of the New World, we came. Transients. Nomads. I bid you welcome."

We all answered back, "Welcome."

The altar boys stood in an arc around the priest as he recited a list of a hundred twenty-nine names, Haitian refugees who had drowned at sea that week. The list was endless and with each name my heart beat faster, for it seemed as though many of those listed might have been people that I had known at some point in my life.

Some of the names sent a wave of sighs and whispers through the group. Occasionally, there was a loud scream.

One woman near the front began to convulse after a man's name was called. It took four people to drag her out of the pew before she hurt herself.

"We make a special call today for a young woman whose name we don't know," the priest said after he had recited all the others. "A young woman who was pregnant when she took a boat from Haiti and then later gave birth to her child on that boat. A few hours after the child was born, its precious life went out, like a candle in a storm, and the mother with her infant in her arms dived into the sea."

There are people in Ville Rose, the village where my mother is from in Haiti, who believe that there are special spots in the sea where lost Africans who jumped off the slave ships still rest, that those who have died at sea have been chosen to make that journey in order to be reunited with their long-lost relations.

During the Mass, Ma tightened a leather belt around her belly, the way some old Haitian women tightened rags around their middles when grieving.

"Think to yourself of the people you have loved and lost," the priest said.

Piercing screams sounded throughout the congregation. Ma got up suddenly and began heading for the aisle. The screams pounded in my head as we left the church.

We walked home through the quiet early morning streets along Avenue D, saying nothing to one another.

· ❖ ·

Caroline was still in bed when we got back.

She wrapped a long black nightgown around her legs as she sat up on a pile of dirty sheets.

There was a stack of cards on a chair by her bed. She picked it up and went through the cards, sorting most of them with one hand and holding the rest in her mouth. She began a game of solitaire using her hand and her lips, flipping the cards back and forth with great agility.

"How was Mass?" she asked.

Often after Mass ended, I would feel as though I had taken a very long walk with the dead.

"Did Ma cry?" she asked.

"We left before she could."

"It's not like she knows these people," Caroline said. Some of the cards slipped from between her lips.

"Ma says all Haitians know each other."

Caroline stacked the cards and dropped them in one of the three large open boxes that were kept lined up behind her bed. She was packing up her things slowly so as to not traumatize Ma.

She and Eric were not going to have a big formal wedding. They were going to have a civil ceremony and then they would take some pictures in the wedding grove at the Brooklyn Botanic Garden. Their honeymoon would be a brief trip to the Bahamas, after which Caroline would move into Eric's apartment.

Ma wanted Eric to officially come and ask her permission to marry her daughter. She wanted him to bring his family to our house and have his father ask her blessing. She wanted Eric to kiss up to her, escort her around, buy her gifts, and shower her with compliments. Ma wanted a full-blown church wedding. She wanted Eric to be Haitian.

"You will never guess what I dreamt last night," Caroline said, dropping her used sheets into one of the moving boxes she was packing. "I dreamt about Papa."

It had been almost ten years since Papa had died of untreated prostrate cancer. After he died, Ma made us wear mourning clothes, nothing but black dresses, for eighteen months. Caroline and I were both in high school at the time, and we quickly found ways to make wearing black a fashion statement. Underneath our black clothes we were supposed to wear red panties. In Ma's family, the widows often wore blood-red panties so that their dead husbands would not come back and lie down next to them at night. Daughters who looked a lot like the widowed mother might wear red panties too so that if they were ever mistaken for her, they would be safe.

Ma believed that Caroline and I would be well protected by the red panties. Papa, and all the other dead men who might desire us, would stay away because the sanguine color of blood was something that daunted and terrified the non-living.

For a few months after Papa died, Caroline and I dreamt of him every other night. It was as though he were taking turns visiting us in our sleep. We would each have the same dream: Papa walking in a deserted field while the two of us were running after him. We were never able to catch up with him because there were miles of saw grass and knee-deep mud between us.

We kept this dream to ourselves because we already knew what Ma would say if we told it to her. She would guess that we had not been wearing our red panties and would warn us that the day we caught up with Papa in our dream would be the day that we both would die.

Later the dreams changed into moments replayed from our lives, times when he had told us stories about his youth in Haiti or evenings when he had awakened us at midnight after working a double shift in his taxicab to take us out for Taste the Tropics ice cream, Sicilian pizzas, or Kentucky Fried Chicken.

Slowly, Papa's death became associated with our black clothes. We began carrying our loss like a medal on our chests, answering every time someone asked why such young attractive girls wore such a somber color, "Our mother makes us do it because our father is dead."

Eighteen months after his death, we were allowed to start wearing other colors, but nothing too bright. We could wear white or gray or navy blue but no orange, or red on the outside. The red for the world to see meant that our mourning period had ended, that we were beyond our grief. The red covering our very private parts was to tell our father that he was dead and we no longer wanted anything to do with him.

"How did you dream of Papa?" I asked Caroline now.

"He was at a party," she said, "with all these beautiful people around him, having a good time. I saw him in this really lavish room. I'm standing in the doorway and he's inside and I'm watching him, and it's like watching someone through a glass window. He doesn't even know I'm there. I call him, but he doesn't answer. I just stand there and watch what he's doing because I realize that he can't see me."

She reached into one of her boxes and pulled out a framed black-and-white picture of Papa, a professional studio photograph taken in the nineteen fifties in Haiti, when Papa was twenty-two. In the photograph, he is wearing a dark suit and tie and has a solemn expression on his face. Caroline looked longingly at the picture, the way war brides look at photographs of their dead husbands. I raised my nightshirt and showed her my black cotton panties, the same type that we had both been wearing since the day our father died. Caroline stuck her pinkie through a tiny hole in the front of my panties. She put Papa's picture back into her box, raised her dress, and showed me her own black panties.

We had *never* worn the red panties that Ma had bought for us over the years to keep our dead father's spirit away. We had always worn our black panties instead, to tell him that he would be welcome to visit us. Even though we no longer wore black outer clothes, we continued to wear black underpants as a sign of lingering grief. Another reason Caroline may have continued to wear hers was her hope that Papa would come to her and say that he approved of her: of her life, of her choices, of her husband.

"With patience, you can see the navel of an ant," I said, recalling one of Papa's favorite Haitian proverbs.

"Rain beats on a dog's skin, but it does not wash out its spots," Caroline responded.

"When the tree is dead, ghosts eat the leaves."

"The dead are always in the wrong."

Beneath the surface of Papa's old proverbs was always some warning.

Our Cuban neighbor, Mrs. Ruiz, was hosting her large extended family in the yard next door after a Sunday christening. They were blasting some rumba music. We could barely hear each other over the crisp staccato pounding of the conga drums and the shrill brass sections blaring from their stereo.

I closed my eyes and tried to imagine their entire clan milling around the yard, a whole exiled family gathering together so far from home. Most of my parents' relatives still lived in Haiti.

Caroline and I walked over to the window to watch the Ruiz clan dance to the rumba.

"Mrs. Ruiz has lost some weight since we saw her last," Caroline said.

"A couple of months ago, Mrs. Ruiz's only son had tried to hijack a plane in Havana to go to Miami. He was shot and killed by the airplane's pilot."

"How do you know such things?" Caroline asked me.

"Ma told me."

When we were younger, Caroline and I would spend all our Sunday mornings in bed wishing that it would be the blessed day that the rest of Caroline's arm would come bursting out of Ma's stomach and float back to her. It would all happen like the brass sections in the Ruizes' best rumbas, a meteoric cartoon explosion, with no blood or pain. After the momentary shock, Caroline would have a whole arm and we would all join Mrs. Ruiz's parties to celebrate. Sometimes Sunday mornings would be so heavy with disappointment that we thought we might explode.

Caroline liked to have her stub stroked. This was something that she had never grown out of. Yet it was the only part of her that people were afraid of. They were afraid of offending her, afraid of staring at it, even while they were stealing a glance or two. A large vein throbbed just below the surface, under a thick layer of skin. I ran my pinkie over the vein and felt it, pulsating against my skin.

"If I slice myself there, I could bleed to death," Caroline said. "Remember what Papa used to say, 'Behind a white cloud, a bird looks like an angel.'"

Ma was in the kitchen cooking our Sunday breakfast when we came in. She was making a thick omelet with dried herring, served with boiled plantains. Something to keep you going as if it were your only meal for the day.

"Mass was nice today," Ma said, watching Caroline balance her orange juice between her chin and her stub. "If you had gone, you would have enjoyed it a lot."

"Yes. I hear it was a ball," Caroline said.

"You two have been speaking for a long time already," Ma said. "What were you discussing?"

"This and that," I said.

"I've been jealous," Ma said.

· ❧ ·

That night I dreamt that I was at a costume ball in an eighteenth-century French chateau, with huge crystal chandeliers above my head. Around me people were wearing masks made from papier-mâché and velvet. Suddenly, one of the men took off his mask. Beneath the mask was my father.

Papa was talking to a group of other people who were also wearing masks. He was laughing as though someone had just told him a really good joke. He turned towards me for a brief second and smiled. I was so happy to see him that I began to cry.

I tried to run to him, but I couldn't. My feet were moving but I was standing in the same place, like a mouse on a treadmill. Papa looked up at me again, and this time he winked. I raised my hand and waved. He waved back. It was a cruel flirtation.

I quickly realized that I would never get near him, so I

stood still and just watched him. He looked much healthier than I remembered, his toasted almond face round and fleshy. I felt as though there was something he wanted to tell me.

Suddenly, he dropped his mask on the ground, and like smoke on a windy day, he disappeared. My feet were now able to move. I walked over to where he had been standing and picked up the mask. The expression on the mask was like a frozen scream. I pressed the mask against my chest, feeling the luxurious touch of velvet against my cheek.

When I looked up again, my father was standing at the foot of a spiral staircase with a group of veiled women all around him. He turned his back to me and started climbing the long winding staircase. The veiled women followed him with their beautiful pink gowns crackling like damp wood in a fire.

Then, the women stopped and turned one by one to face me, slowly raising their veils. As they uncovered their faces, I realized that one of them, standing tall and rigid at Papa's side, was Caroline.

Of the two of us, Caroline was the one who looked most like Papa. Caroline looked so much like Papa that Ma liked to say they were *one head on two bodies, Tèt koupe.*

I started screaming at the top of my lungs. Why were they leaving me out? I should have been there with them.

I woke up with my face soaked with tears, clutching my pillow.

That morning, I wrote down a list of things that I remembered having learned from my father. I had to remind myself, at least under my breath, that I did remember still. In the back of my mind, I could almost hear his voice saying these things to me, in the very same way that he had spoken over the years: "You have memory of walking in a mist at dawn in a banana jungle that no longer exists. You have lived this long in this strange world, so far from home, because you remember."

The lifelines in my father's palms were named after Caroline and me. He remembered everything. He remembered old men napping on tree branches, forgetting the height of the trees and the vulnerability of their bodies. He remembered old women sitting sidesaddle on ancient donkeys, taking their last steps. He remembered young wives who got ill from sadness when their men went to the Bahamas or the Dominican Republic to cut sugarcane and were never heard from again. These women lived in houses where they slept on sugar sacks on the floor, with mourning ropes around their bellies, houses where the marital bed was never used again and where the middle pillar was sacred.

He remembered never-ending flour fogs in the country marketplace, fogs that folks compared to the inside of a crazy woman's head. He remembered calling strangers "Mother," "Sister", "Brother," because his village's Creole demanded a family title for everyone he addressed.

My father had memories of eating potato, breadfruit, and avocado peels that he was supposed to be feeding to his mother's pigs. He remembered praying for the rain to stay away even during drought season because his house had a hole in the roof right above his cot. Later he felt guilty that there was no crop, because he thought that it was his prayers that had kept away the rain.

He remembered hearing his illiterate mother reciting

poetry and speaking in a tongue that sounded like Latin when she was very ill with typhoid fever. This was the time he tried to stuff red hot peppers into his mother's nose because he was convinced that if the old woman sneezed three times, she would live.

It was my father's job to look for the falling star that would signal his mother's impending death, and when he saw it crash in a flash behind the hills above his house, he screamed and howled like a hurt dog. After his mother died, he stuffed live snakes into bottles to imprison his anger. He swam in waterfalls with healing powers. He piled large rocks around his mother's house to keep the dead spirit in the ground. He played King of the Mountain on garbage heaps. He trapped fireflies in matchboxes so he would not inhale them in his sleep. He collected beads from the braids in his mother's hair and swallowed them in secret so he would always have a piece of her inside of him. And even when he was in America, he never looked at a night sky again.

"I have a riddle for you. Can you handle it?" he would ask.

"Bring it on. Try me."

"Ten thousand very large men are standing under one small umbrella. How is it that none of them gets wet?"

"It is not raining."

"Why is it that when you lose something, it is always in the very last place you look?"

"Because once you find it, you look no more."

He had a favorite joke: God once called a conference of world leaders. He invited the president of France, the president of the United States, the president of Russia, Italy, Germany, and China, as well as our own president, His Excellency, the

President for Life Papa Doc Duvalier. When the president of France reached the gates of Heaven, God got up from his throne to greet him. When the president of the United States reached the gates of Heaven, God got up to greet him as well. So, too, with the presidents of Russia, Italy, Germany, and China.

When it was our president's turn, His Excellency, the President for Life Papa Doc Duvalier, God did not get up from his throne to greet him. All the angels were stunned and puzzled. They did not understand God's very rude behavior. So they elected a representative to go up to God and question Him.

"God," said the representative, "you have been so cordial to all the other presidents. You have gotten up from your throne to greet them at the gates of Heaven as soon as they have entered. Why do you not get up for Papa Doc Duvalier? Is it because he is a black president? You have always told us to overlook the color of men. Why have you chosen to treat the black president, Papa Doc Duvalier, in this fashion?"

God looked at the representative angel as though He was about to admit something that He did not want to.

"Look," he said. "I am not getting up for Papa Doc Duvalier because I am afraid that if I get up, he will take my throne and will never give it back."

These were our bedtime stories. Tales that haunted our parents and made them laugh at the same time. We never understood them until we were fully grown and they became our sole inheritance.

· ❖ ·

Caroline's wedding was only a month away. She was very matter-of-fact about it, but slowly we all began to prepare. She had bought a short white dress at a Goodwill thrift shop and paid twelve dollars to dry-clean it. Ma, too, had a special dress: a pink lace, ankle-sweeping evening gown that she was going to wear at high noon to a civil ceremony. I decided to wear a green suit, for hope, like the handkerchief that wrapped Ma's marriage proposal letter from Papa's family.

Ma would have liked to have sewn Caroline's wedding dress from ten different patterns in a bridal magazine, taking the sleeves from one dress, the collar from another, and the skirt from another. Though in her heart she did not want to attend, in spite of everything, she was planning to act like this was a real wedding.

"The daughter resents a mother forever who keeps her from her love," Ma said as we dressed to go to Eric's house for dinner. "She is my child. You don't cut off your own finger because it smells bad."

Still, she was not going to cook a wedding-night dinner. She was not even going to buy Caroline a special sleeping gown for her "first" sexual act with her husband.

"I want to give you a wedding shower," I said to Caroline in the cab on the way to Eric's house.

There was no sense in trying to keep it a secret from her.

"I don't really like showers," Caroline said, "but I'll let you give me one because there are certain things that I need."

She handed me her address book, filled mostly with the names of people at Jackie Robinson Intermediate School where we both taught English as a Second Language to Haitian students.

Eric and Caroline had met at the school, where he was a janitor. They had been friends for at least a year before he asked her out. Caroline couldn't believe that he wanted to go out with her. They dated for eighteen months before he asked her to marry him.

"A shower is like begging," Ma said, staring out of the car window at the storefronts along Flatbush Avenue. "It is even more like begging if your sister gives one for you."

"The maid of honor is the one to do it," I said. "I am the maid of honor, Ma. Remember?"

"Of course I remember," she said. "I am the mother, but that gives me claim to nothing."

"It will be fun," I tried to assure her. "We'll have it at the house."

"Is there something that's like a shower in Haiti?" Caroline asked Ma.

"In Haiti we are poor," Ma said, "but we do not beg."

· ❦ ·

"It's nice to see you, Mrs. Azile," Eric said when he came to the door.

Eric had eyes like Haitian lizards, bright copper with a tint of jade. He was just a little taller than Caroline, his rich mahogany skin slightly darker than hers.

Under my mother's glare, he gave Caroline a timid peck on the cheek, then wrapped his arms around me and gave me a bear hug.

"How have you been?" Ma asked him with her best, extreme English pronunciation.

"I can't complain," he said.

Ma moved over to the living room couch and sat down in front of the television screen. There was a nature program playing without sound. Mute images of animals swallowing each other whole flickered across the screen.

"So, you are a citizen of America now?" Eric said to me. "Now you can just get on a plane anytime you feel like it and go anywhere in the world. Nations go to war over women like you. You're an American."

His speech was extremely slow on account of a learning disability.

Ma looked around the room at some carnival posters on Eric's living room wall. She pushed her head forward to get a better look at a woman in a glittering bikini with a crown of feathers on her head. Her eyes narrowed as they rested on a small picture of Caroline, propped in a silver frame on top of the television set.

Eric and Caroline disappeared in the kitchen, leaving me alone with Ma.

"I won't eat if it's bad," she said.

"You know Eric's a great cook," I said.

"Men cooking?" she said. "There is always something wrong with what he makes, here or at our house."

"Well, pretend to enjoy it, will you?"

She walked around the living room, picking up the small wooden sculptures that Eric had in many corners of the room, mostly brown Madonnas with caramel babies wrapped in their arms.

Eric served us chicken in a thick dark sauce. I thrust my fork through layers of gravy. Ma pushed the food around her plate but ate very little.

After dinner, Eric and Caroline did the dishes in the kitchen while Ma and I sat in front of the television.

"Did you have a nice time?" I asked her.

"Nice or not nice, I came," she said.

"That's right, Ma. It counts a lot that you came, but it would have helped if you had eaten more."

"I was not very hungry," she said.

"That means you can't fix anything to eat when you get home," I said. "Nothing. You can't fix anything. Not even bone soup."

"A woman my age in her own home following orders."

Eric had failed miserably at the game of Wooing Haitian Mother-in-Law. Had he known—or rather had Caroline advised him well—he would have hired a Haitian cook to make Ma some Haitian food that would taste (God forbid!) even better than her own.

· ❧ ·

"We know people by their stories," Ma said to Caroline in the cab on the way home that night. "Gossip goes very far. Grace heard women gossip in the Mass behind us the other day, and you hear what they say about Haitian women who forget themselves when they come here. Value yourself."

"Yes, Ma," Caroline said, for once not putting up a fight.

I knew she wanted to stay and spend the night with Eric but she was sparing Ma.

"I can't accuse you of anything," Ma said. "You never call someone a thief unless you catch them stealing."

"I hear you, Ma," Caroline said, as though her mind were a thousand miles away.

When we got home, she waited for Ma to fall asleep, then called a car service and went back to Eric's. When I got up the next morning, Ma was standing over my bed.

"Did your sister leave for school early again?" she asked.

"Yes, Ma," I said. "Caroline is just like you. She sleeps a hair thread away from waking, and she rises with the roosters."

· ❧ ·

I mailed out the invitations for Caroline's wedding shower. We kept the list down to a bare minimum, just a few friends and Mrs. Ruiz. We invited none of Ma's friends from Saint Agnes because she told me that she would be ashamed to have them ask her the name of her daughter's fiancé and have her tongue trip, being unable to pronounce it.

"What's so hard about Eric Abrahams?" I asked her. "It's practically a Haitian name."

"But it isn't a Haitian name," she said. "The way I say it is not the way his parents intended for it to be said. I say it Haitian. It is not Haitian."

"People here pronounce our names wrong all the time."

"That is why I know the way I say his name is not how it is meant to be said."

"You better learn his name. Soon it will be your daughter's."

"That will never be my daughter's name," she said, "because it was not the way I intended her name to be said."

In the corner behind her bed, Caroline's boxes were getting full.

"Do you think Ma knows where I am those nights when I'm not here?" she asked.

"If she caught you going out the door, what could she do? It would be like an ant trying to stop a flood."

"It's not like I have no intention of getting married," she said.

"Maybe she understands."

That night, I dreamed of my father again. I was standing on top of a cliff, and he was leaning out of a helicopter trying to grab my hand. At times, the helicopter flew so low that it nearly knocked me off the cliff. My father began to climb down a plastic ladder hanging from the bottom of the helicopter. He was dangling precariously and I was terrified.

I couldn't see his face, but I was sure he was coming to rescue me from the top of that cliff. He was shouting loudly, calling out my name. He called me Gracina, my full Haitian name, not Grace, which is what I'm called here.

It was the first time in any of my dreams that my father had a voice. The same scratchy voice that he had when he was alive. I stretched my hands over my head to make it easier for him to reach me. Our fingers came closer with each swing of the helicopter. His fingertips nearly touched mine as I woke up.

When I was a little girl, there was a time that Caroline and I were sleeping in the same bed with our parents because we had eaten beans for dinner and then slept on our backs, a combination that gives bad dreams. Even though she was in our parents' bed, Caroline woke up in the middle of the night, terrified. As she sobbed, Papa rocked her in the dark, trying to console her. His face was the first one she saw when Ma turned on the light. Looking straight at Papa with dazed eyes, Caroline asked him, "Who are you?"

He said, "It's Papi."

"Papi who?" she asked.

"Your papi," he said.

"I don't have a papi," she said.

Then she jumped into Papa's arms and went right back to sleep.

My mother and father stayed up trying to figure out what made her say those things.

"Maybe she dreamt that you were gone and that she was sleeping with her husband, who was her only comfort," Ma said to Papa.

"So young, she would dream this?" asked Papa.

"In dreams we travel the years," Ma had said.

Papa eventually went back to sleep, but Ma stayed up all night thinking.

The next day she went all the way to New Jersey to get Caroline fresh bones for a soup.

"So young she would dream this," Papa kept saying as he watched Caroline drink the soup. "So young. Just look at her, our child of the promised land, our New York child, the child who has never known Haiti."

I, on the other hand, was the first child, the one they called their "misery baby," the offspring of my parents' lean years.

I was born to them at a time when they were living in a shantytown in Port-au-Prince and had nothing.

When I was a baby, my mother worried that I would die from colic and hunger. My father pulled heavy carts for pennies. My mother sold jugs of water from the public fountain, charcoal, and grilled peanuts to get us something to eat.

When I was born, they felt a sense of helplessness. What if the children kept coming like the millions of flies constantly buzzing around them? What would they do then? Papa would need to pull more carts. Ma would need to sell more water, more charcoal, more peanuts. They had to try to find a way to leave Haiti.

Papa got a visa by taking vows in a false marriage with a widow who was leaving Haiti to come to the United States. He gave her some money and she took our last name. A few years later, my father divorced the woman and sent for my mother and me. While my father was alive, this was something that Caroline and I were never supposed to know.

· ❖ ·

We decorated the living room for Caroline's shower. Pink streamers and balloons draped down from the ceiling with the words *Happy Shower* emblazoned on them.

Ma made some patties from ground beef and codfish. She called one of her friends from Saint Agnes to bake the shower cake cheap. We didn't tell her friend what the cake was for. Ma wrote Caroline's name and the date on it after it had been delivered. She scrubbed the whole house, just in case one of the strangers wanted to use our bathroom. There wasn't a trace of dirt left on the wallpaper, the tiles, even the bathroom cabinets. If cleanliness is next to godliness, then whenever we had company my mother became a goddess.

Aside from Ma and me, there were only a few other people at the shower: four women from the junior high school where we taught and Mrs. Ruiz.

Ma acted like a waitress and served everyone as Caroline took center stage sitting on the loveseat that we designated the "shower chair." She was wearing one of her minidresses, a navy blue with a wide butterfly collar. We laid the presents in front of her to open, after she had guessed what was inside.

"Next a baby shower!" shouted Mrs. Ruiz in her heavy Spanish accent.

"Let's take one thing at a time," I said.

"Never too soon to start planning," Mrs. Ruiz said. "I promise to deliver the little one myself. Caroline, tell me now, what would you like, a girl or a boy?"

"Let's get through one shower first," Caroline said.

I followed Ma to the kitchen as she picked up yet another empty tray.

"Why don't you sit down for a while and let me serve?" I asked Ma as she put another batch of patties in the oven. She looked like she was going to cry.

When it was time to open the presents, Ma stayed in the kitchen while we all sat in a circle watching Caroline open her gifts.

She got a juicer, a portable step exerciser, and some other household appliances from the schoolteachers. I gave her a traveling bag to take on her honeymoon.

Ma peeked through the doorway as we cooed over the appliances, suggesting romantic uses for them: breakfasts in bed, candlelight dinners, and the like. Ma pulled her head back quickly and went into the kitchen.

She was in the living room to serve the cake when the time came for it. While we ate, she gathered all of the boxes and the torn wrapping paper and took them to the trash bin outside.

She was at the door telling our guests good-bye as they left.

"Believe me, Mrs. Azile, I will deliver your first grand-child," Mrs. Ruiz told her as she was leaving.

"I am sorry about your son," I said to Mrs. Ruiz.

"Now why would you want to bring up a thing like that?" Mrs. Ruiz asked.

"Carmen, next time you come I will give you some of my bone soup," Ma said as Mrs. Ruiz left.

Ma gave me a harsh look as though I had stepped out of line in offering my belated condolences to Mrs. Ruiz.

"There are things that don't always need to be said," Ma told me.

· ❄ ·

Caroline packed her gifts before going to bed that night. The boxes were nearly full now.

We heard a knock on the door of our room as we changed for bed. It was Ma in her nightgown holding a gift-wrapped package in her hand. She glanced at Caroline's boxes in the corner, quickly handing Caroline the present.

"It is very sweet of you to get me something," Caroline said, kissing Ma on the cheek to say thank you.

"It's very nothing," Ma said, "very nothing at all."

Ma turned her face away as Caroline lifted the present out of the box. It was a black and gold silk teddy with a plunging neckline.

'At the store," Ma said, "I told them your age and how you would be having this type of a shower. A girl there said that this would make a good gift for such things. I hope it will be of use."

"I like it very much," Caroline said, replacing it in the box.

After Caroline went to bed, I went to Ma's room for one of our chats. I slipped under the covers next to her, the way Caroline and I had come to her and Papa when our dreams had frightened us.

"That was nice, the teddy you got for Caroline," I said. "But it doesn't seem much like your taste."

"I can't live in this country twenty-five years and not have some of it rub off on me," she said. "When will I have to buy you one of those dishonorable things?"

"When you find me a man."

"They can't be that hard to find," she said. "Look, your sister found one, and some people might think it would be harder for her. He is a retard, but that's okay."

"He's not a retard, Ma. She found a man with a good heart."

"Maybe."

"You like him, Ma. I know deep inside you do."

"After Caroline was born, your father and me, we were so afraid of this."

"Of what?"

"Of what is happening."

"And what is that?"

"Maybe she jumps at it because she thinks he is being noble. Maybe she thinks he is doing her a favor. Maybe she thinks he is the only man who will ever come along to marry her."

"Maybe he loves her," I said.

"Love cannot make horses fly," she said. "Caroline should not marry a man if that man wants to be noble by marrying Caroline."

"We don't know that, Ma."

"The heart is like a stone," she said. "We never know what it is in the middle.

"Only some hearts are like that," I said.

"That is where we make mistakes," she said. "All hearts are stone until we melt, and then they turn back to stone again."

"Did you feel that way when Papa married that woman?" I asked.

"My heart has a store of painful marks," she said, "and that is one of them."

Ma got up from the bed and walked over to the closet with all her suitcases. She pulled out an old brown leather bag filled with tiny holes where the closet mice had nibbled at it over the years.

She laid the bag on her bed, taking out many of the items that she had first put in it years ago when she left Haiti to come to the United States to be reunited with my father.

She had cassettes and letters written by my father, his words crunched between the lines of aging sheets of ruled loose-leaf paper. In the letters he wrote from America to her while she was still in Haiti, he never talked to her about love.

He asked about practical things; he asked about me and told her how much money he was sending her and how much was designated for what.

My mother also had the letters that she wrote back to him, telling him how much she loved him and how she hoped that they would be together soon.

That night Ma and I sat in her room with all those things around us. Things that we could neither throw away nor keep in plain sight.

· ❀ ·

Caroline seemed distant the night before her wedding. Ma made her a stew with spinach, yams, potatoes, and dumplings. Ma did not eat any of the stew, concentrating instead on a green salad, fishing beneath the lettuce leaves as though there was gold hidden on the plate.

After dinner, we sat around the kitchen radio listening to a music program on the Brooklyn Haitian station.

Ma's lips were moving almost unconsciously as she mouthed the words to an old sorrowful bolero. Ma was putting the final touches on her own gown for the wedding.

"Did you check your dress?" she asked Caroline.

"I know it fits," Caroline said.

"When was the last time you tried it on?"

"Yesterday."

"And you didn't let us see it on you? I could make some adjustments."

"It fits, Ma. Believe me."

"Go and put it on now," Ma said.

"Maybe later."

"Later will be tomorrow," Ma said.

"I will try it on for you before I go to sleep," Caroline promised.

Ma gave Caroline some ginger tea, adding two large spoonfuls of brown sugar to the cup.

"You can learn a few things from the sugarcane," Ma said to Caroline. "Remember that in your marriage."

"I didn't think I would ever fall in love with anybody, much less have them marry me," Caroline said, her fingernails tickling the back of Ma's neck.

"Tell me, how do these outside-of-church weddings work?" Ma asked.

"Ma, I told you my reasons for getting married this way," Caroline said. "Eric and I don't want to spend all the money we have on one silly night that everybody else will enjoy except us. We would rather do it this way. We have all our papers ready. Eric has a friend who is a judge. He will perform the ceremony for us in his office."

"So much like America," Ma said, shaking her head. "Everything mechanical. When you were young, every time someone asked you what you wanted to do when you were all grown up, you said you wanted to marry Pelé. What's happened to that dream?"

"Pelé who?" Caroline grimaced.

"On the eve of your wedding day, you denounce him, but you wanted to marry him, the Brazilian soccer player; you always said when you were young that you wanted to marry him."

I was the one who wanted to marry Pelé. When I was a little girl, my entire notion of love was to marry the soccer star. I would confess it to Papa every time we watched a game together on television.

In our living room, the music was dying down as the radio station announced two A.M. Ma kept her head down as she added a few last stitches to her dress for the wedding.

"When you are pregnant," Ma said to Caroline, "give your body whatever it wants. You don't want your child to have port-wine marks from your cravings."

Caroline went to our room and came back wearing her wedding dress *and* a prosthetic arm.

Ma's eyes wandered between the bare knees poking beneath the dress and the device attached to Caroline's forearm.

"I went out today and got myself a wedding present," Caroline said. It was a robotic arm with two shoulder straps that controlled the motion of the plastic fingers.

"Lately, I've been having this shooting pain in my stub and it feels like my arm is hurting," Caroline said.

"It does not look very real," Ma said.

"That's not the point, Ma!" Caroline snapped.

"I don't understand," Ma said.

"I often feel a shooting pain at the end of my left arm, always as though it was cut from me yesterday. The doctor said I have phantom pain."

"What? The pain of ghosts?"

"Phantom limb pain," Caroline explained, "a kind of pain that people feel after they've had their arms or legs amputated. The doctor thought this would make it go away."

"But your arm was never cut from you," Ma said. "Did you tell him that it was God who made you this way?"

"With all the pressure lately, with the wedding, he says that it's only natural that I should feel amputated."

"In that case, we all have phantom pain," Ma said.

· ❧ ·

When she woke up on her wedding day, Caroline looked drowsy and frazzled, as if she had aged several years since the last time we saw her. She said nothing to us in the kitchen as she swallowed two aspirins with a gulp of water.

"Do you want me to make you some soup?" Ma asked.

Caroline said nothing, letting her body drift down into Ma's arms as though she were an invalid. I helped her into a chair at the kitchen table. Ma went into the hall closet and pulled out some old leaves that she had been saving. She stuffed the leaves into a pot of water until the water overflowed.

Caroline was sitting so still that Ma raised her index finger under her nose to make sure she was breathing.

"What do you feel?" Ma asked.

"I am tired," Caroline said. "I want to sleep. Can I go back to bed?"

"The bed won't be yours for much longer," Ma said. "As soon as you leave, we will take out your bed. From this day on, you will be sleeping with your husband, away from here."

"What's the matter?" I asked Caroline.

"I don't know," she said. "I just woke up feeling like I don't want to get married. All this pain, all this pain in my arm makes it seem so impossible somehow."

"You're just nervous," I said.

"Don't worry," Ma said. "I was the same on the morning

of my wedding. I fell into a stupor, frightened of all the possibilities. We will give you a bath and then you lay down for a bit and you will rise as promised and get married."

The house smelled like a forest as the leaves boiled on the stove. Ma filled the bathtub with water and then dumped the boiled leaves inside.

We undressed Caroline and guided her to the tub, helping her raise her legs to get in.

"Just sink your whole body," Ma said, when Caroline was in the tub.

Caroline pushed her head against the side of the tub and lay there as her legs paddled playfully towards the water's surface.

Ma's eyes were fierce with purpose as she tried to stir Caroline out of her stupor.

"At last a sign," she joked. "She is my daughter after all. This is just the way I was on the day of my wedding."

Caroline groaned as Ma ran the leaves over her skin.

"Woman is angel," Ma said to Caroline. "You must confess, this is like pleasure."

Caroline sank deeper into the tub as she listened to Ma's voice.

"Some angels climb to heaven backwards," Caroline said. "I want to stay with us, Ma."

"You take your vows in sickness and in health," Ma said. "You decide to try sickness first? That is not very smart."

"You said this happened to you too, Ma?" Caroline asked.

"It did," Ma said. "My limbs all went dead on my wedding day. I vomited all over my wedding dress on the way to the church."

"I am glad I bought a cheap dress then," Caroline said, laughing. "How did you stop vomiting?"

"My honeymoon."

"You weren't afraid of that?"

"Heavens no," Ma said, scrubbing Caroline's back with a handful of leaves. "For that I couldn't wait."

Caroline leaned back in the water and closed her eyes.

"I am eager to be a guest in your house," Ma said to Caroline.

"I will cook all your favorite things," Caroline said.

"As long as your husband is not the cook, I will eat okay."

"Do you think I'll make a good wife, Ma?"

"Even though you are an island girl with one kind of season in your blood, you will make a wife for all seasons: spring, summer, autumn, and winter."

Caroline got up from the tub and walked alone to Ma's bedroom.

The phone rang and Ma picked it up. It was Eric.

"I don't understand it, honey," Caroline said, already sounding more lucid. "I just felt really blah! I know. I know, but for now, Ma's taking care of me."

· ❁ ·

Ma made her hair into tiny braids, and over them she put on a wig with a shoulder-length bob. Ma and I checked ourselves in the mirror. She in her pink dress and me in my green suit, the two of us looking like a giant patchwork quilt.

"How long do I have now?" Caroline asked.

"An hour," I said.

"Eric is meeting us there," Caroline said, "since it's bad luck for the groom to see the bride before the wedding."

"If the groom is not supposed to see the bride, how do they get married?" Ma asked.

"They're not supposed to see each other until the ceremony," Caroline said.

Caroline dressed quickly. Her hair was slicked back in a small bun, and after much persuasion, Ma got her to wear a pair of white stockings to cover her jutting knees.

The robotic arm was not as noticeable as the first time we had seen it. She had bought a pair of long white gloves to wear over the prosthetic arm and her other arm. Ma put some blush on the apple of Caroline's cheeks and then applied some rice powder to her face. Caroline sat stiffly on the edge of her bed as Ma glued fake eyelashes to her eyelids.

I took advantage of our last few minutes together to snap some instant Polaroid memories. Caroline wrapped her arms tightly around Ma as they posed for the pictures.

"Ma, you look so sweet," Caroline said.

We took a cab to the courthouse. I made Ma and Caroline pose for more pictures on the steps. It was as though we were going to a graduation ceremony.

· ❀ ·

The judge's secretary took us to a conference room while her boss finished an important telephone call.

Eric was already there, waiting. As soon as we walked in, Eric rushed over to give Caroline a hug. He began stroking her prosthetic arm as though it were a fascinating new toy.

"Lovely," he said.

"It's just for the day," Caroline said.

"It suits you fine," he said.

Caroline looked much better. The rouge and rice powder had given her face a silky brown-sugar finish.

Ma sat stiffly in one of the cushioned chairs with her purse in her lap, her body closed in on itself like a cage.

"Judge Perez will be right with you," the secretary said.

Judge Perez bounced in cheerfully after her. He had a veil of thinning brown hair and a goatee framing his lips.

"I'm sorry the bride and groom had to wait," he said giving Eric a hug. "I couldn't get off the phone."

"Do you two know what you're getting into?" he said, playfully tapping Eric's arm.

Eric gave a coy smile. He wanted to move on with the ceremony. Caroline's lips were trembling with a mixture of fear and bashfulness.

"It's really a simple thing," Judge Perez said. "It's like a visit to get your vaccination. Believe me when I tell you it's very short and painless."

He walked to a coat rack in the corner, took a black robe from it, and put it on.

"Come forward, you two," he said, moving to the side of the room. "The others can stand anywhere you like."

Ma and I crowded behind the two of them. Eric had no family here. They were either in another state or in the Bahamas.

"No best man?" Ma whispered.

"I'm not traditional," Eric said.

"That wasn't meant to be heard," Ma said, almost as an apology.

"It's all right," Eric said.

"Dearly beloved," Judge Perez began. "We are gathered here today to join this man and this woman in holy matrimony."

Caroline's face, as I had known it, slowly began to fade, piece by piece, before my eyes. Another woman was setting in, a married woman, someone who was no longer my little sister.

"I, Caroline Azile, take this man to be my lawful wedded husband."

I couldn't help but feel as though she was divorcing us, trading in her old allegiances for a new one.

· ❈ ·

It was over before we knew it. Eric grabbed Caroline and kissed her as soon as the judge said, "Her lips are yours."

"They were mine before, too," Eric said, kissing Caroline another time.

After the kiss, they stood there, wondering what to do next. Caroline looked down at her finger, admiring her wedding band. Ma took a twenty-dollar bill out of her purse and handed it to the judge. He moved her hand away, but she kept insisting. I reached over and took the money from Ma's hand.

"I want to take the bride and groom out for a nice lunch," I said.

"Our plane leaves for Nassau at five," Eric said.

"We'd really like that, right, Ma?" I said. "Lunch with the bride and groom."

Ma didn't move. She understood the extent to which we were unimportant now.

"I feel much better," Caroline said.

"Congratulations, Sister," I said. "We're going to take you out to eat."

"I want to go to the Brooklyn Botanic Garden to take some pictures," Caroline said.

"All set," Eric said. "I have a photographer meeting us there."

Ma said, "How come you never told me you were leaving tonight? How come you never tell me nothing."

"You knew she wasn't going back to sleep at the house with us," I said to Ma.

"I am not talking to you," Ma said, taking her anger out on me.

"I am going to stop by the house to pick up my suitcase," Caroline said.

· ❧ ·

We had lunch at Le Bistro, a Haitian Restaurant on Flatbush Avenue. It was the middle of the afternoon, so we had the whole place to ourselves. Ma sat next to me, not saying a word. Caroline didn't eat very much either. She drank nothing but sugared water while keeping her eyes on Ma.

"There's someone out there for everyone," Eric said, standing up with a champagne glass in the middle of the empty restaurant. "Even some destined bachelors get married. I am a very lucky person."

Caroline clapped. Ma and I raised our glasses for his toast.

He and Caroline laughed together with an ease that Ma and I couldn't feel.

"Say something for your sister," Ma said in my ear.

I stood up and held my glass in her direction.

"A few years ago, our parents made this journey," I said. "This is a stop on the journey where my sister leaves us. We will miss her greatly, but she will never be gone from us."

It was something that Ma might have said.

· ❀ ·

The photographer met us at the wedding grove at the Botanic Garden. Eric and Caroline posed stiffly for their photos, surrounded by well-cropped foliage.

"These are the kinds of pictures that they will later lay over the image of a champagne glass or something," Ma said. "They do so many tricks with photography now, for posterity."

We went back to the house to get Caroline's luggage.

"We cannot take you to the airport," Ma said.

"It's all right, Mother," Eric said. "We will take a cab. We will be fine."

I didn't know how long I held Caroline in my arms on the sidewalk in front of our house. Her prosthetic arm felt weighty on my shoulder, her hair stuck to the tears on my face.

"I'll visit you and Ma when I come back," she said. "Just don't go running off with any Brazilian soccer players."

Caroline and I were both sobbing by the time she walked over to say good-bye to Ma. She kissed Ma on the cheek and then quickly hopped in the taxi without looking back. Ma ran her hand over the window, her finger sliding along the car door as it pulled away.

"I like how you stood up and spoke for your sister," she said.

"The toast?"

"It was good."

"I feel like I had some help," I said.

· ❀ ·

That night, Ma got a delivery of roses so red that they didn't look real.

"Too expensive," she said when the delivery man handed them to her.

The guy waited for her to sign a piece of paper and then a bit longer for a tip.

Ma took a dollar out of her bra and handed it to him.

She kept sniffing the roses as she walked back to the kitchen.

"Who are they from?" I asked.

"Caroline," she said. "Sweet, sweet Caroline."

Distance had already made my sister Saint Sweet Caroline.

"Are you convinced of Caroline's happiness now?" I asked.

"You ask such difficult questions."

That night she went to bed with a few Polaroids of the wedding photos and the roses by her bed. Later, I saw her walking past my room cradling the vase. She woke up several times to sniff the roses and change the water.

That night, I also dreamt that I was with my father by

a stream of rose-colored blood. We made a fire and grilled a breadfruit for dinner while waiting for the stream to turn white. My father and I were sitting on opposite sides of the fire. Suddenly the moon slipped through a cloud and dived into the bloody stream, filling it with a sheet of stars.

I turned to him and said, "Look, Papi. There are so many stars."

And my father in his throaty voice said, "If you close your eyes really tight, wherever you are, you will see these stars."

I said, "Let's go for a swim."

He said, "No, we have a long way to travel and the trip will be harder if we get wet."

Then I said, "Papa, do you see all the blood? It's very beautiful."

His face began to glow as though it had become like one of the stars.

Then he asked me, "If we were painters, which landscapes would we paint?"

I said, "I don't understand."

He said, "We are playing a game, you must answer me."

I said, "I don't know the answers."

"When you become mothers, how will you name your sons?"

"We'll name them all after you," I said.

"You have forgotten how to play this game," he said.

"What kind of lullabies do we sing to our children at night? Where do you bury your dead?"

His face was fading into a dreamy glow.

"What kind of legends will your daughters be told? What kinds of charms will you give them to ward off evil?"

I woke up startled, for the first time afraid of the father that I saw in my dreams.

I rubbed the sleep out of my eyes and went down to the kitchen to get a glass of warm milk.

Ma was sitting at the kitchen table, rolling an egg between her palms. I slipped into the chair across from her. She pressed harder on both ends of the egg.

"What are you doing up so late?" she asked.

"I can't sleep," I said.

"I think people should take shifts. Some of us would carry on at night and some during the day. The night would be like the day exactly. All stores would be open and people would go to the office, but only the night people. You see, then there would be no sleeplessness."

I warmed some cold milk in a pan on the stove. Ma was still pressing hard, trying to crush the egg from top and bottom. I offered her some warm milk but she refused.

"What did you think of the wedding today?" I asked.

"When your father left me and you behind in Haiti to move to this country and marry that woman to get our papers," she said, "I prepared a charm for him. I wrote his name on a piece of paper and put the paper in a calabash. I filled the calabash with honey and next to it lit a candle. At midnight every night, I laid the calabash next to me in the bed where your father used to sleep and shouted at it to love me. I don't know how or what I was looking for, but somehow in the words he was sending me, I knew he had stopped thinking of me the same way."

"You can't believe that, Ma," I said.

"I know what I know," she said. "I am an adult woman. I am not telling you this story for pity."

The kitchen radio was playing an old classic on one of the Haitian stations.

Beloved Haiti, there is no place like you.

I had to leave you before I could understand you.

"Would you like to see my proposal letter?" Ma asked.

She slid an old jewelry box across the table towards me. I opened it and pulled out the envelope with the letter in it.

The envelope was so yellowed and frail that at first I was afraid to touch it.

"Go ahead," she said, "it will not turn to dust in your hands."

The letter was cracked along the lines where it had been folded all of these years.

My son, Carl Romélus Azile, would be honored to make your daughter, Hermine Françoise Génie, his wife.

"It was so sweet then," Ma said, "so sweet. Promise me that when I die you will destroy all of this."

"I can't promise you that," I said. "I will want to hold on to things when you die. I will want to hold on to you."

"I do not want my grandchildren to feel sorry for me," she said. "The past, it fades a person. And yes. Today, it was a nice wedding."

· ❀ ·

My passport came in the mail the next day, addressed to Gracina Azile, my real and permanent name.

I filled out all the necessary sections, my name and address, and listed my mother to be contacted in case I was in an accident. For the first time in my life, I felt truly secure living in America. It was like being in a war zone and finally receiving a weapon of my own, like standing on the firing line and finally getting a bulletproof vest.

We had all paid dearly for this piece of paper, this final assurance that I belonged in the club. It had cost my parents' marriage, my mother's spirit, my sister's arm.

I felt like an indentured servant who had finally been allowed to join the family.

. ❧ .

The next morning, I went to the cemetery in Rosedale, Queens, where my father had been buried. His was one of many gray tombstones in a line of foreign unpronounceable names. I brought my passport for him to see, laying it on the grass among the wild daisies surrounding the grave.

"Caroline had her wedding," I said. "We felt like you were there."

My father had wanted to be buried in Haiti, but at the time of his death there was no way that we could have afforded it.

The day before Papa's funeral, Caroline and I had told Ma that we wanted to be among Papa's pallbearers.

Ma had thought that it was a bad idea. Who had ever heard of young women being pallbearers? Papa's funeral was no time for us to express our selfish childishness, our *American* rebelliousness.

When we were children, whenever we rejected symbols of Haitian culture, Ma used to excuse us with great embarrassment and say, "You know, they are American."

Why didn't we like the thick fatty pig skin that she would

deep-fry so long that it tasted like rubber? We were Americans and we had *no taste buds*. A double tragedy.

Why didn't we like the thick yellow pumpkin soup that she spent all New Year's Eve making so that we would have it on New Year's Day to celebrate Haitian Independence Day? Again, because we were American and the Fourth of July was *our* independence holiday.

"In Haiti, you own your children and they find it natural," she would say. "They know their duties to the family and they act accordingly. In America, no one owns anything, and certainly not another person."

. ❊ .

"Caroline called," Ma said. She was standing over the stove making some bone soup when I got home from the cemetery. "I told her that we would still keep her bed here for her, if she ever wants to use it. She will come and visit us soon. I knew she would miss us."

"Can I drop one bone in your soup?" I asked Ma.

"It is your soup too," she said.

She let me drop one bone into the boiling water. The water splashed my hand, leaving a red mark.

"Ma, if we were painters which landscapes would we paint?" I asked her.

"I see. You want to play the game of questions?"

"When I become a mother, how will I name my daughter?"

"If you want to play then I should ask the first question," she said.

"What kinds of lullabies will I sing at night? What kinds of legends will my daughter be told? What kinds of charms will I give her to ward off evil?"

"I have come a few years further than you," she insisted. "I have tasted a lot more salt. I am to ask the first question, if we are to play the game."

"Go ahead," I said giving in.

She thought about it for a long time while stirring the bones in our soup.

"Why is it that when you lose something, it is always in the last place that you look for it?" she asked finally.

Because of course, once you remember, you always stop looking.

Epilogue: Women Like Us

· ❖ ❖ ❖ ·

· ❖ ❖ ❖ ·

You remember thinking while braiding your hair that you look a lot like your mother. Your mother who looked like your grandmother and her grandmother before her. Your mother had two rules for living. *Always use your ten fingers,* which in her parlance meant that you should be the best little cook and housekeeper who ever lived.

Your mother's second rule went along with the first. Never have sex before marriage, and even after you marry, you shouldn't say you enjoy it, or your husband won't respect you.

And writing? Writing was as forbidden as dark rouge on the cheeks or a first date before eighteen. It was an act of indolence, something to be done in a corner when you could have been learning to cook.

Are there women who both cook and write? Kitchen poets, they call them. They slip phrases into their stew and wrap meaning around their pork before frying it. They make narrative dumplings and stuff their daughter's mouths so they say nothing more.

"What will she do? What will be her passion?" your aunts would ask when they came over to cook on great holidays, which called for cannon salutes back home but meant nothing at all here.

"Her passion is being quiet," your mother would say. "But then she's not being quiet. You hear this scraping from her. Krik? Krak! Pencil, paper. It sounds like someone crying."

Someone was crying. You and the writing demons in your head. You have nobody, nothing but this piece of paper, they told you. Only a notebook made out of discarded fish wrappers, panty-hose cardboard. They were the best confidantes for a lonely little girl.

When you write, it's like braiding your hair. Taking a handful of coarse unruly strands and attempting to bring them unity. Your fingers have still not perfected the task. Some of the braids are long, others are short. Some are thick, others are thin. Some are heavy. Others are light. Like the diverse women in your family. Those whose fables and metaphors, whose similes, and soliloquies, whose diction and *je ne sais quoi* daily slip into your survival soup, by way of their fingers.

You have always had your ten fingers. They curse you each time you force them around the contours of a pen.

No, women like you don't write. They carve onion sculptures and potato statues. They sit in dark corners and braid their hair in new shapes and twists in order to control the stiffness, the unruliness, the rebelliousness.

· ❧ ·

You remember thinking while braiding your hair that you look a lot like your mother. You remember her silence when you laid your first notebook in front of her. Her disappointment when you told her that words would be your life's work, like the kitchen had always been hers. She was angry at you for not understanding. *And with what do you repay me? With scribbles on paper that are not worth the scratch of a pig's snout.* The sacrifices had been too great.

Writers don't leave any mark in the world. Not the world where we are from. In our world, writers are tortured and killed if they are men. Called lying whores, then raped and killed, if they are women. In our world, if you write, you are a politician, and we know what happens to politicians. They end up in a prison dungeon where their bodies are covered in scalding tar before they're forced to eat their own waste.

The family needs a nurse, not a prisoner. We need to forge ahead with our heads raised, not buried in scraps of throwaway paper. We do not want to bend over a dusty grave, wearing black hats, grieving for you. There are nine hundred and ninety-nine women who went before you and worked their fingers to coconut rind so you can stand here before me holding that torn old notebook that you cradle against your breast like your prettiest Sunday braids. I would rather you had spit in my face.

You remember thinking while braiding your hair that you look a lot like your mother and her mother before her. It was their whispers that pushed you, their murmurs over pots sizzling in your head. A thousand women urging you to speak through the blunt tip of your pencil. Kitchen poets, you call them. Ghosts like burnished branches on a flame tree. These women, they asked for your voice so that they could tell your mother in your place that yes, women like you do speak, even if they speak in a tongue that is hard to understand. Even if it's patois, dialect, Creole.

. ❧ .

The women in your family have never lost touch with one another. Death is a path we take to meet on the other side. What goddesses have joined, let no one cast asunder. With every step you take, there is an army of women watching over you. We are never any farther than the sweat on your brows or the dust on your toes.

Though you walk through the valley of the shadow of death, fear no evil for we are always with you.

. ❧ .

When you were a little girl, you used to dream that you were lying among the dead and all the spirits were begging you to scream. And even now, you are still afraid to dream because you know that you will never be able to do what they say, as they say it, the old spirits that live in your blood.

Most of the women in your life had their heads down. They would wake up one morning to find their panties gone. It is not shame, however, that kept their heads down. They were singing, searching for meaning in the dust. And sometimes, they were talking to faces across the ages, faces like yours and mine.

You thought that if you didn't tell the stories, the sky would fall on your head. You often thought that without the trees, the sky would fall on your head. You learned in school that you have pencils and paper only because the trees gave themselves in unconditional sacrifice. There have been days when the sky was as close as your hair to falling on your head.

This fragile sky has terrified you your whole life. Silence terrifies you more than the pounding of a million pieces of steel chopping away at your flesh. Sometimes, you dream of hearing only the beating of your own heart, but this has never been the case. You have never been able to escape the pounding of a thousand other hearts that have outlived yours by thousands of years. And over the years when you have needed us, you have always cried "Krik?" and we have answered "Krak!" and it has shown us that you have not forgotten us.

. ❊ .

You remember thinking while braiding your hair that you look a lot like your mother. Your mother, who looked like your grandmother and her grandmother before her. Your mother, she introduced you to the first echoes of the tongue that you now speak when at the end of the day she would braid your hair while you sat between her legs, scrubbing the kitchen pots. While your fingers worked away at the last shadows of her day's work, she would make your braids Sunday-pretty, even during the week.

When she was done she would ask you to name each braid after those nine hundred and ninety-nine women who were boiling in your blood, and since you had written them down and memorized them, the names would come rolling off your tongue. And this was your testament to the way that these women lived and died and lived again.

New to the Twentieth Anniversary Edition

In the Old Days

· ❄ ❄ ❄ ·

. ❧ ❧ ❧ .

The call came on a Friday evening as I was lying in bed, grading student essays.

"My husband," the sniffling woman on the other end of the line said, "is dying and it seems that . . ." She paused and it sounded as though she was swallowing more air than she wanted to. "And it seems that his final wish is to spend a few minutes with you."

Once these words were out of the way, the woman's voice grew a tad more firm, raspy, but still confident, as she immediately turned to the logistical details.

"Time," she said, "is of course of the essence. We would fly you over on the earliest New York–Miami flight possible. My husband is still here at home. Of course we can get you a hotel room nearby. The house is small, but big enough that you could stay with us if you like."

The woman's husband was my father, but I had never met him. I know only one side of the story: my mother's.

My father had returned to Haiti during what he'd

considered a promising time for the country. A thirty-year father-son dictatorship had just ended and he wanted to use the education degree he'd managed to get during the day, while working as a busboy in an Italian restaurant in the evenings, to start a school there. My mother stayed behind in Brooklyn, promising to join him a few weeks later. Instead she discovered she was pregnant with me and shipped him divorce papers.

"I'm not sure I can just drop everything," I told my father's wife that Friday evening. "I have school."

"On the weekend?" she asked.

"On the usual," I answered.

"So you're a student?" she asked.

"A teacher like him."

"What do you teach?" she asked.

"High school," I said

"What subject?"

"Books," I said. "I mean English."

At that point it was obvious that we were both trying way too hard.

"Please come see him," she said.

"I don't know," I said.

But I already knew I would.

· ❧ ·

I didn't jump on the next flight though, like someone with nothing better to do, like someone who'd been waiting for that phone call her entire life. Instead I continued grading my students' papers, which were not really essays, but my ninth graders' initial—I had asked for primal—reactions to a piece of literature that they had voted on as a class to read. I had given them a choice between the school's limited options, Carson McCullers's *The Member of the Wedding* or Albert Camus's *The Stranger*, and being recent strangers themselves to both English and to America, the majority of them voted for *The Stranger*.

"WHAT?" began one boy's reaction paper. "I don't think I'd be so kalm if my moms died."

Before the phone rang, I had scribbled "AMEN BROTHER!" in red ink, in the margin of his single-spaced stream-of-consciousness masterpiece, but after hanging up, I wrote him a long note scolding him for oversimplifying and being careless with his spelling, then I gave him an F.

. ❖ .

"Already she got in touch with you," my mother said when I met her at Nadia's, a Haitian restaurant that she had started a year after I was born, and had also named after me. We were sitting at our table, a corner one for two, which allowed her a view of the entire place, from the customers' entrance, through the bar, to the kitchen. Above our heads was one of my mother's paintings, which covered the restaurant walls, our home, and nowhere else. Most of my mother's paintings were trompe l'œils—à la Magritte, as she liked to say—in which the subject, person or thing, always seemed to be trying to escape the frame. The one above our table, the one that marked our spot, was the restaurant's signature painting. It was of a plum brown baby girl swimming in a large bowl of pumpkin soup that seemed to be spilling out of the round frame.

The place was packed because a popular *konpa* band had a ten o'clock show scheduled at the reception hall next door and some older couples in sequined dresses and tuxedos stopped in for dinner first. Usually my mother would be running around between the storeroom and her office, grabbing meat out of the freezer and bottles out of the wine cellar, acting as maître d', hostess, or waitress as needed, but when I told her about the call, she walked me over to our table and told me to sit down.

This corner, this table, had been in my life for as long as I could remember. It was where I napped in my car seat, where I learned to color between the lines, where I did my homework and read hundreds and hundreds of books, as my mother worked. It was the only spot where she could see me wherever she was in the restaurant, and over the years I had grown to love it.

I had also grown to love the fact that there was never any background music piped through the speakers at Nadia's, because while sitting at that table, I overheard conversations that surpassed the drama in many of the books I was reading. I witnessed and was sometimes invited to join christening and baptism parties, communion and wedding lunches, graduation dinners, wakes and funeral receptions. I heard men and women declare their love for each other then listened as others confessed that they had fallen out of love. I heard parents explain the birds and the bees to their kids then leaned forward as a girl at another table revealed to her mother and father that she was pregnant or a boy announced to his parents that he had knocked up someone's daughter. Why did so many people think that they could confess the most shocking things to each other over a meal? Had they been biding their time, waiting for a moment when the other person was sitting in a public place with a mouth full of food and couldn't scream? I saw parents announce to their bawling children that they were divorcing. I heard women reveal to men that the children they'd raised were not theirs and elderly parents inform grown sons and daughters that they were disowning them. But I had never heard anyone announce to their twenty-four-year-old daughter, as my mother had the week before, that the father she'd previously been told had abandoned her hadn't even known that she existed.

My mother has always been a fast speaker. She often spoke as though she was on her way somewhere. Even her customers, offering lavish praise and seeking details about the food, could not get her to linger in conversation. The only unhurried thing about her was how she put together her clothes. She liked clingy wraparound dresses with plunging necklines, black silk and lace slips, which I sometimes borrowed and wore as outdoor clothing. I was wearing one of those slip dresses when the call came and decided to wear it to the restaurant even though it was still the early part of spring and most people were wearing long sleeves, even indoors. I felt most beautiful when my mother's patrons complimented her on her beauty, because in the next breath, they would also say I looked like her.

My mother had concluded our conversation the week before by saying, "An old friend told me that he's very sick. I asked my friend to pass on your number to his wife." And how did this happen, I wondered. Did she simply tell the friend, "Oh by the way, he has a daughter and here's his daughter's number"?

It was second nature for my mother to survey the dining room, her eyes never resting on one thing for too long. She was literally itching to get away from me, clawing her elbows with well-manicured fingernails.

"Please go see him," she was saying now, even as she waved hello to someone walking through the front door.

I tried to imagine the child me, observing this: two nearly identical-looking women sitting with their backs stiffened and attached to fancy cushioned chairs that maybe they were both hoping had an electric switch that someone might turn on at any time to put them out of their misery. Or was it wrong of me to think of death in a jokey manner, when the person who might want to turn on that switch—at least my mother's switch—was actually in the process of dying?

One of the waiters carried over two Prestige beers with napkins wrapped around the cold, sweating bottle. Once the waiter put the beers down, my mother motioned with her head for him to step away from the table and leave us alone.

"As I told you last week," my mother said, grabbing her beer, "in the old days, we were not the only ones. Many marriages fell apart when the dictatorship ended. There was suddenly a hard line between those who wanted to go back and *swa dizan* rebuild the country and those of us who decided to stay out for good."

She put the beer down and with wet, broken napkin pieces still stuck to her palm, covered her face with her hands and breathed long and hard into them as though they were a paper bag. When she pulled her hands away, I realized that she was crying.

I reached over and picked out tiny clumps of wet paper from her cheeks. As I leaned in, my mother's slip of a dress suddenly felt too small and too frail on me and I felt ridiculously underdressed. Was I too much my mother's daughter, wired not only with the same taste, but also the same fears?

"He still chose a country over us," she said, digging her fingers past her plaited braids into her scalp.

"Maybe he would have made a different choice if he'd known about me." I was on the verge of yelling, even if it lost my mother business. This is why, I realized, we were talking out in the dining room and not in her office. She knew that being out in public would keep me from being loud.

"Don't you want to see him too?" I asked.

"I didn't see him live," she said, rising from our table. "Why would I want to see him die?"

. ❖ .

I wasn't sure why it surprised me that my father's wife was not at the airport to pick me up the next afternoon.

"I can't leave him alone now," she said abruptly on the phone.

I had only been to Miami once before, two years earlier, on vacation with a now ex-boyfriend. We had stayed in a small hotel by the beach and spent most of our time swimming in the ocean. Miami to me was the beach. Now it would be the place where I would meet my father.

The house was on a corner between rusting, deactivated train tracks and a long line of ancient, majestic-looking oak trees. A tall concrete wall surrounded the property with a metal gate on the side. I rang the bell at the side gate a few times before a buzzer signaled that I could push it open.

Both the yard and the house were smaller than the wall might suggest. A short trail led through a cluster of cabbage palms towards the front door, where my father's wife was waiting. She was wearing a purple caftan that, when she raised her arms to greet me, filled up the entire doorframe. On each of her bare feet was a string of cowry shells and small bells that chimed as she moved towards me. She raised her glasses and rested them on her short afro, then looking over my gray sweat suit and overstuffed handbag, asked, "Is this all you brought?"

The little bells kept chiming as I followed her through a dark foyer into the living room. The living room decor was sparse, with a velvet brown pull-out sofa and a matching ottoman and a TV console covered with adult diapers and unwrapped syringes.

My father's wife motioned for me to sit down on the sofa while she crouched down on the ottoman. Given the twenty-year age difference between him and my mother, I wasn't surprised that this wife too was relatively young. Looking down at her feet, my father's wife said, "The chimes? You're curious about the chimes. They're so he could hear me, sort of, wherever I am in the house."

So this was the Earth Mother that had replaced mine.

"I'm sure you have a lot of questions," she said.

"Can I see him?" I asked.

"You could," she said, "but maybe you want to talk first, to prepare yourself."

She got up and the bells came to life again. "We both need a drink," she said, then disappeared down a narrow hallway leading to the rest of the house. I felt slightly lightheaded. My stomach, empty since the night before—except for the couple of glasses of wine I've had on the plane—was now churning with both hunger and anxiety. The chimes grew faint until I stopped hearing them altogether, then they would start up again then stop, then start again. This is not a sound I would want to hear all day if I were dying, but then that's just me.

When she came back, my father's wife handed me a tall glass of something that smelled as though it had rum in it. I gulped it down like it was lemonade to keep from having to engage in any more conversation. She followed suit, pouring herself a glass from a pitcher she laid down on a side table next to me. This made me think that maybe the drink wasn't as potent as I'd initially thought, so I poured myself another glass. I thought I heard people whispering, in the distance, then nearby.

"Is there anyone else here?" I asked, looking around. The walls seemed to be closing in. I half expected someone—my father?—to come out and throw the diapers on the TV console at me while scolding me, irrationally, for staying away so long.

"Easy," my father's wife said, flashing what seemed a more and more beautiful smile. "We're both nervous, but let's go easy on the drink."

"Amen, sister," I wanted to say, but remained quiet.

After a while, from somewhere deep at the bottom of the second glass came the courage for me to ask "So where did you two kids meet?"

"Me and Marc?"

"Yes, you and Marc." I shouted out "Marc" hoping it would force my father to come out and greet me, but even my own voice was beginning to sound foreign to me.

"Marc and I met through some friends in Haiti," she was saying, her voice growing slower and slower by the second.

"Are you a teacher too?" I asked.

"I'm a lawyer." She pushed her head towards mine, narrowing her eyes as though she was worried about me. "After the dictatorship ended," she proceeded cautiously, pausing between her words, "I went back to see what I could do. I was working with a group that was trying to rebuild the justice system. The head of the group introduced me to Marc."

Marc. I was slowly getting used to the name. Marc. My father's name was Marc. Marc with a different last name than mine.

"Do you have any children?" I asked her.

"Me and Marc?"

I nodded, though I meant her alone. Maybe she was like my mother. Maybe all women were like my mother, concealers of secret children.

"No children," she said, "but I left my first husband behind."

"No children that you know of," I said, then let out a cackle loud enough to drown out the sound of her ankle bells.

"You have your father's sense of humor," she said in a voice that suddenly became even slower and deeper, "though I'm afraid you won't get to see that because many things about him have been stripped away."

"How do you mean?" I asked. "Is he able to talk?"

"You could talk to him if you like," she said. "I still speak to him. I think I will always speak to him."

She closed her eyes for a moment as if to illustrate how they would speak. Telepathically? In her dreams?

"When did he—you two—get back to the States?" I asked.

"A few weeks ago," she said, "after his condition worsened. We're lucky some friends were able to let us use this house."

"What exactly is wrong with him?" I asked.

"At this stage, it really doesn't matter," she said. "It's irreversible."

At our confession dinner the week before, I had asked my mother what she remembered most about my father.

"His seriousness," she'd said. "He never said anything he didn't mean."

"Do you think you made a difference there?" I asked my father's wife, "In Haiti I mean?"

"You mean was it worth it, sacrificing so much, leaving so much behind to go and try to save Haiti?"

There was still traffic coming the other way, I wanted to remind her, for example, the teenagers I was teaching now, whose parents were still fleeing the country—uneducated and without justice—decades after she and my father and people like them had gone there to educate everyone and give them justice.

"Did you two ever think about having children together?" I asked.

"'Take care of one child or a few hundreds, which would

you choose?' That's what Marc used to tell me when we talked about having our own children."

When she noticed me reaching for the empty glass as if hoping it would magically fill up again, she said, "I am sorry. I didn't always agree with him on that. Or his approach to you."

So he had known about me. The bastard had known, as some of my students would say. And still he had decided not to come back. He had chosen a country over us, as my mother had said, because it was nobler to take care of hundreds than one, or hundreds *and* one.

I was suddenly thirsty, very thirsty, like I had just swallowed a gallon of sea water. Then my mouth felt dry. Still I managed to say, "How can he have asked for me to come here if you say he's not even talking?"

"He didn't," she said. "I did. He was already too far along to know much when I got your information from your mother and Marc's friends."

So they had tricks, as my students would say. My father, her, my mother. They all had tricks. They were super slick. I was fake smiling for I don't know how long. My father's wife was fake smiling too. Then my mouth started aching and I felt as though I was going to vomit.

"I really would like to see him," I heard myself say. Maybe so I could slap his face. Maybe so I could beat him up, finish him off myself.

"You will see him," she said, as the room began to fade and emerge again, flying needles, adult diapers, floating around in the haze that was now my mind.

The ankle bells grew louder as she approached me until it seemed as though they were ringing inside my head. I leaned back into the sofa and floated down towards it. Then I remembered something from my F student's paper. He was angry at me for making him read, but he was also angrier with Camus, with Meursault, *The Stranger*, for saying that deep down it didn't matter whether you died at thirty or seventy years old.

"Hell yeah it does," he'd closed his paper with. "Every sekond kount."

I promised myself that I would raise his grade when I got back.

"Before you see your father, come meet some folks," my father's wife then said.

"So there are other people here?" I said.

"Friends," she said.

I leaned on the ottoman next to the couch for support as I got up. The hall light was on. Even though my legs were a bit wobbly, I followed a long narrow hallway to the kitchen where a small group of people, three men and three women, were sitting around a square table, each silently clutching a glass of that same lemonade-seeming drink. A bottle of Barbancourt rum was in the middle of the table.

Seeing the rum reminded me how much I would have loved another drink if only I wasn't so hungry, so angry, and now also foggy.

"You didn't have much in your stomach when you took those drinks, did you?" my father's wife said, while standing at my side in front of everyone.

"I'm a cheap date," I mumbled.

She then turned to everyone at the table and said, "Everybody, this is Marc's daughter, Nadia. She's visiting from New York."

If they were shocked that Marc had a daughter Nadia who lived in New York, they did not show it.

"Nadia, these are friends of mine and Marc's," she said. Then she went around introducing each of them. One of them was a doctor. She barely looked older than me. Assuming that we were two of the youngest people there, I felt a sudden allegiance to her. She was wearing a dark pant suit, no doctor's coat or scrubs, but had a stethoscope around her neck.

"I'll just be a minute," she said, after my father's wife reintroduced her as his hospice physician. The hospice physician then walked further down the hall to what I assumed was my father's room.

My father's wife then pointed to the collared minister among the remaining five and said, "Pastor brought Marc to Christ before it was too late."

I gave an extra nod to the minister, who got up from his chair so I could sit in it. As he pulled out the chair for me, he said, "This must be a great shock."

"Marc and Nadia have not spent much time together," my father's wife said.

"Or any at all," I said.

I couldn't believe that I had been in that house that long and had not seen the man himself. I felt the minister's hands stroke my shoulder. "Can I see him now?" I asked.

"Have some soup," my father's wife said.

She walked over to the stove and poured me a bowl of what was actually a stew filled with dumplings and greens.

"I made it myself," said one of the women around the table, "and there's plenty more if you need it."

As I slurped my way through the stew, the minister put his

hands on my shoulders again. The others linked hands and bowed their heads.

"Let's pray for Nadia," the minister said.

I wondered why they were praying for me and not my father, but like the stew, the prayer calmed my stomach.

. ❧ .

"You can go in now," the hospice doctor told us all when she returned to the kitchen.

I wanted to see my father alone, without the small congregation as witnesses, so I asked for another bowl of stew and drank it slowly while they walked to him singing a mournful hymn.

> *Shall we gather at the river?*
> *The beautiful, beautiful river*

The doctor was standing at the kitchen counter, typing something into a laptop as I finished a third bowl of stew. When it seemed like they were never coming out, I followed the singing into my father's room.

The room was dim, save for a desk lamp on a table filled with gauze and ointments and other medical supplies. On the other side, where everyone was standing, was a small cot covered with an eyelet-embroidered white sheet. My father's bed was directly beneath a ceiling fan, which was circulating cold air from a stand-alone air-conditioning unit on a side window. I was freezing.

My father's wife stepped aside and left a space open at the

foot of the bed. Before my father left for Haiti, my mother had told me at our confession dinner, she had pretended that she was going to join him and had made him pack everything in a container, including every picture she ever had of him, even their wedding picture. So I had nothing to compare the skeletal man lying on a hospital bed to, except my own face. From the outline of his stiff, pajama clad body under the thin blanket, I could see that we were about the same height, though the illness might have shrunk him. If there was any territory for me to claim, it had to be on his face. I had to find myself in his drawn-out coppery skin, in the uneven rise of his forehead, in the tightly sealed eyes, the eyebrows that had nearly disappeared, the deep pockets beneath the hollow cheeks, the clenched jaws and gray peach fuzz on his chin.

I let my hands travel up the frigid railing of the hospital bed towards my father's face, which when my fingertips grazed it felt as prickly and haggard as it looked and just as dead. I pressed my palm down on his forehead and it was almost slippery, like a well-polished mask. I kept thinking I could peel his skin off if I wanted to, all the way down his cranium towards the back of his neck.

I turned to my father's wife for an explanation. She had her back turned to me, her face pressed against the minister's chest, and was quietly sobbing. Her sobs reminded me of my mother's tears, even though they were crying over two different men, neither of whom I knew.

I pulled my hand away from my father's face as his friends streamed out of the room, one by one, slowly and carefully, as if hoping I wouldn't notice. My father's wife and I were now alone with him, both our pelvises pressed against the bed's railing.

"For him, this is the kind of freedom that people always talk about for those who are suffering," my father's wife said.

I wasn't sure I understood.

"He is gone now," she said. "He is free. We rejoice for his freedom." Even as she said this, her face was distorted with as much agony as horror. "He died right before you arrived," she finally admitted.

In her flushed and swollen features, I could see the void that my father had left. I could see it as clearly as though it were a gash, a wound, a scar. I was desperate to feel what she was feeling. I was envying it, coveting it.

"Why couldn't you tell me when I walked in?" I asked.

She was now standing in the same position as when she'd been using the minister as a leaning post; her arms were raised, her head bowed. Why was the minister even there? Did she not trust me to meet my father's corpse alone?

"There is no rush now," she said, "no emergency. The doctor will pronounce him dead when you tell her to, when you are ready. He's been out of it for the past day or so, but we were told he could still hear us, until the moment he stopped breathing."

So officially, at least on paper, my father was still not dead.

How would I one day describe this my own child, I thought, if ever I had one? How would I describe it to my mother? My mother who thought that nothing having to do with my father was in the present, that everything involving him was in the past, in the old days, in *her* old days.

In the old days, she had told me at that confession

dinner—perhaps when they'd all lived in one small village that never was—in the old days, she'd said, church bells chimed for each person who died. In the old days when a baby was born, the midwife would put the baby on the ground, on a blanket, in front of the father's feet, and it was up to the father to bend down and pick up the child and claim the child as his own. In the old days, the dead were kept at home. In the old days, I, the oldest daughter, would have been given some comforting rum-filled brew, or salted black coffee, to drink before seeing her father's body for the first time. These would have been some of the measures taken to protect me from *sezisman*, or total, crippling shock. In the old days, I would have pronounced my father dead with my wails and cries to his fellow villagers. Looking down at my father's dead face, in which I saw no trace of my own, I wanted him to get up and explain to me *his* version of the old days.

"Please forgive him," my father's wife said. "But I know he would have wanted this. I know he would have wanted you to be part of the final rituals. Please forgive him. Please forgive us. There is no rush now. You can take your time here, then we will declare him dead."

My father's wife then walked out of the room, which was suddenly brighter when she opened the door allowing some of the hallway light in.

I sat down on the cot that was meant for my father's wife, the cot where she must have spent many nights on both a vigil and a deathwatch. Sitting closer to the floor, where I was staring at the metal feet of the bed and not at my father's face, I felt even colder. I pushed my head back and pressed my spine against the eyelet sheet. I wanted to close my eyes, but I couldn't take them off the fan that was twirling over my head. Somehow it reminded me of wanting to put my hands into another type of fan in my mother's restaurant when I was little and seeing if it would really cut them off as my mother had told me it would.

Out in the hall, I heard my father's wife and her friends talking. They were speaking in low voices, perhaps thinking that they were whispering when they were not.

After a very long prayer, the minister said, "Surely a simple service would do, then the cremation, just as he'd asked."

Then they began singing. They sang about gathering by rivers, beautiful, beautiful rivers, with bright angels and crystal tides. They sang about hearts quivering and pilgrimages ceasing. And during a still moment where neither prayer nor song could be heard, I heard the doctor say, "How much longer do you think the daughter will be in there?"

The daughter? She had said the daughter. And the daughter was me.

The daughter will be in there about a day, a month, a year, I thought. She will be in there in the short span of the lifetime she'd been allowed. How about the daughter just stay in here forever? But even if I weren't a stranger, even if we'd spent our entire lives together, I wouldn't be able to stay in there with my father forever. So I got up and walked back over to the hospital bed, then bent down and pressed my lips against my father's cold forehead. I did this because somehow I think it would have been expected of me. If he had been awake when I'd arrived, this is also what I would have done.

My father did not look like he was sleeping. A sliver of white was now visible underneath his eyelids. An entire world seemed to be hiding there, a world I had never been privy to, a world I would never know.

I straightened myself up. It would have been simpler perhaps and easier to cry, to even want to cry, to mourn things I had no idea I'd lost, to wonder how I would ever be able to live without him.

"*Aurevoir*, Papa," I said, trying the word out just this once. I had always wondered what it would be like to call someone Papa. I had even imagined my mother remarrying so I could do it. This, I realized, would be the first and last time I would ever say it to the man that had actually been my father.

I turned my back on all of this, on him, and started walking towards the door. I kept expecting something to stop me, a hand on my shoulder, a whisper that would reverse if not my entire life, than this incomplete moment. But my father did not wake up, nor did he call my name.

Aujourd'hui, papa est mort.

My father died today.

As I walked out the bedroom door, my father's wife's ankle bells began to chime. The chimes were headed in my direction. Softly at first, then louder and more persistent, as though she were not just walking, but jumping up and down, in a way that sounded, strangely, like joy.

I would like to dedicate this book to the memory of my aunts Josephine and Marie-Rose who both passed away this year. Your love and guidance will always be with us. Many thanks to my mother and father for continued support. Thanks to the folks at the Brown University Creative Writing program, especially Karen Davies, Gale Nelson, Meredith Steinbach, Robert Coover, Paula Vogel, Thadious Davis, Aishah Rahman, and Rosemarie Waldrop, who were the first to see these stories. Thank you, Ann Birstein and Elizabeth Dalton. I owe so much to Melanie Fleishman for all your very hard work, to the wonderful gang at Clinica who became like family to me, to Jonathan and Ed for giving me a chance to learn so much about myself. To my aunt Grace and my cousin Magalie Adonis, my cousins Betty and Mendy, Esther for the braids, and to Nadine Gilles, sister of the yam. And to Paule Marshall, the greatest kitchen poet of all.

—Edwidge Danticat, 1995

· ❀ ❀ ❀ ·

EDWIDGE DANTICAT is the author of numerous books, including *Brother, I'm Dying*, which won the National Book Critics Circle Award and was a National Book Award finalist; *Breath, Eyes, Memory*, an Oprah Book Club selection; *Krik? Krak!*, a National Book Award finalist; and *The Dew Breaker*, winner of the inaugural Story Prize. The recipient of a MacArthur Fellowship, she has been published in *The New Yorker*, *The New York Times*, and elsewhere. *The Farming of Bones* won an American Book Award for fiction in 1999.

Continue reading for a preview of Edwidge Danticat's

BREATH,
EYES, MEMORY

1

· ❧ ❧ ❧ ·

A flattened and drying daffodil was dangling off the little card that I had made my aunt Atie for Mother's Day. I pressed my palm over the flower and squashed it against the plain beige cardboard. When I turned the corner near the house, I saw her sitting in an old rocker in the yard, staring at a group of children crushing dried yellow leaves into the ground. The leaves had been left in the sun to dry. They would be burned that night at the *konbit* potluck dinner.

I put the card back in my pocket before I got to the yard. When Tante Atie saw me, she raised the piece of white cloth she was embroidering and waved it at me. When I stood in front of her, she opened her arms just wide enough for my body to fit into them.

"How was school?" she asked, with a big smile.

She bent down and kissed my forehead, then pulled me down onto her lap.

"School was all right," I said. "I like everything but those reading classes they let parents come to in the afternoon.

· 1 ·

Everybody's parents come except you. I never have anyone to read with, so Monsieur Augustin always pairs me off with an old lady who wants to learn her letters, but does not have children at the school."

"I do not want a pack of children teaching me how to read," she said. "The young should learn from the old. Not the other way. Besides, I have work."

A blush of embarrassment rose to her brown cheeks.

"At one time, I would have given anything to be in school. But not at my age. My time is gone. Cooking and cleaning, looking after others, that's my school now. That schoolhouse is your school. Cutting cane was the only thing for a young one to do when I was your age. That is why I never want to hear you complain about *your* school." She adjusted a pink head rag wrapped tightly around her head and dashed off a quick smile revealing two missing side teeth. "As long as you do not have to work in the fields, it does not matter that I will never learn to read that ragged old Bible under my pillow."

Whenever she was sad, Tante Atie would talk about the sugar cane fields, where she and my mother practically lived when they were children. They saw people die there from sunstroke every day. Tante Atie said that, one day while they were all working together, her father—my grandfather— stopped to wipe his forehead, leaned forward, and died. My grandmother took the body in her arms and tried to scream the life back into it. They all kept screaming and hollering, as my grandmother's tears bathed the corpse's face. Nothing would bring my grandfather back.

. ❖ .

The *bòlèt* man was coming up the road. He was tall and yellow like an amber roach. The children across the road lined up by the fence to watch him, clutching one another as he whistled and strolled past them.

This albino, whose name was Chabin, was the biggest lottery agent in the village. He was thought to have certain gifts that had nothing to do with the lottery, but which Tante Atie believed put the spirits on his side. For example, if anyone was chasing him, he could turn into a snake with one flip of his tongue. Sometimes, he could see the future by looking into your eyes, unless you closed your soul to him by thinking of a religious song and prayer while in his presence.

I could tell that Tante Atie was thinking of one of her favorite verses as he approached. *Death is the shepherd of man and in the final dawn, good will be the master of evil.*

"*Onè, mes belles*, Atie, Sophie."

Chabin winked at us from the front gate. He had no eyelashes—or seemed to have none. His eyebrows were tawny and fine like corn silk, but he had a thick head of dirty red hair.

"How are you today?" he asked.

"Today, we are fine," Tante Atie said. "We do not know about tomorrow."

"*Ki nimewo* today?" he asked. "What numbers you playing?"

"Today, we play my sister Martine's age," Tante Atie said. "Sophie's mother's age. Thirty-one. Perhaps it will bring me luck."

"Thirty-one will cost you fifty cents," he said.

Tante Atie reached into her bra and pulled out one gourde.

"We will play the number twice," she said.

Even though Tante Atie played faithfully, she had never won at the *bòlèt*. Not even a small amount, not even once.

She said the lottery was like love. Providence was not with her, but she was patient.

The albino wrote us a receipt with the numbers and the amount Tante Atie had given him.

The children cringed behind the gate as he went on his way. Tante Atie raised her receipt towards the sun to see it better.

"There, he wrote your name," I said pointing to the letters, "and there, he wrote the number thirty-one."

She ran her fingers over the numbers as though they were quilted on the paper.

"Would it not be wonderful to read?" I said for what must have been the hundredth time.

"I tell you, my time is passed. School is not for people my age."

The children across the street were piling up the leaves in Madame Augustin's yard. The bigger ones waited on line as the smaller ones dropped onto the pile, bouncing to their feet, shrieking and laughing. They called one another's names: Foi, Hope, Faith, Espérance, Beloved, God-Given, My Joy, First Born, Last Born, Aséfi, Enough-Girls, Enough-Boys, Délivrance, Small Misery, Big Misery, No Misery. Names as bright and colorful as the giant poincianas in Madame Augustin's garden.

They grabbed one another and fell to the ground,

rejoicing as though they had flown past the towering flame trees that shielded the yard from the hot Haitian sun.

"You think these children would be kind to their mothers and clean up those leaves," Tante Atie said. "Instead, they are making a bigger mess."

"They should know better," I said, secretly wishing that I too could swim in their sea of dry leaves.

Tante Atie threw her arms around me and squeezed me so hard that the lemon-scented perfume, which she dabbed across her chest each morning, began to tickle my nose.

"Sunday is Mother's Day, *non?*" she said, loudly sucking her teeth. "The young ones, they should show their mothers they want to help them. What you see in your children today, it tells you about what they will do for you when you are close to the grave."

I appreciated Tante Atie, but maybe I did not show it enough. Maybe she wanted to be a real mother, have a real daughter to wear matching clothes with, hold hands and learn to read with.

"Mother's Day will make you sad, won't it, Tante Atie?"

"Why do you say that?" she asked.

"You look like someone who is going to be sad."

"You were always wise beyond your years, just like your mother."

She gently held my waist as I climbed down from her lap. Then she cupped her face in both palms, her elbows digging into the pleats of her pink skirt.

I was going to sneak the card under her pillow Saturday night so that she would find it as she was making the bed on Sunday morning. But the way her face drooped into her palms made me want to give it to her right then.

I dug into my pocket, and handed it to her. Inside was a poem that I had written for her.

She took the card from my hand. The flower nearly fell off. She pressed the tape against the short stem, forced the baby daffodil back in its place, and handed the card back to me. She did not even look inside.

"Not this year," she said.

"Why not this year?"

"Sophie, it is not mine. It is your mother's. We must send it to your mother."

I only knew my mother from the picture on the night table by Tante Atie's pillow. She waved from inside the frame with a wide grin on her face and a large flower in her hair. She witnessed everything that went on in the house, each step, each stumble, each hug and kiss. She saw us when we got up, when we went to sleep, when we laughed, when we got upset at each other. Her expression never changed. Her grin never went away.

I sometimes saw my mother in my dreams. She would chase me through a field of wildflowers as tall as the sky. When she caught me, she would try to squeeze me into the small frame so I could be in the picture with her. I would scream and scream until my voice gave out, then Tante Atie would come and save me from her grasp.

I slipped the card back in my pocket and got up to go inside. Tante Atie lowered her head and covered her face with her hands. Her fingers muffled her voice as she spoke.

"When I am done feeling bad, I will come in and we will find you a very nice envelope for your card. Maybe it will get to your mother after the fact, but she will welcome it because it will come directly from you."

"It is your card," I insisted.

"It is for a mother, your mother." She motioned me away with a wave of her hand. "When it is Aunt's Day, you can make me one."

"Will you let me read it to you?"

"It is not for me to hear, my angel. It is for your mother."

I plucked out the flower and dropped it under my shoes. Then I put the card back in my pocket.

Across the road, the children were yelling each other's names, inviting passing friends to join them. They sat in a circle and shot the crackling leaves high above their heads. The leaves landed on their faces and clung to their hair. It was almost as though they were caught in a rain of daffodils.

I continued to watch the children as Tante Atie prepared what she was bringing to the potluck. She put the last touches on a large tray of sweet potato pudding that filled the whole house with its molasses scent.

As soon as the sun set, lamps were lit all over our quarter. The smaller children sat playing marbles near whatever light they could find. The older boys huddled in small groups near the school yard fence as they chatted over their books. The girls formed circles around their grandmothers' feet, learning to sew.

Tante Atie had promised that in another year or so she would teach me how to sew.

"You should not stare," she said as we passed a near-sighted old woman whispering mystical secrets of needle and thread to a little girl. The girl was squinting as her eyes dashed back and forth to keep up with the movements of her grandmother's old fingers.

"Can I start sewing soon?" I asked Tante Atie.

"Soon as I have a little time," she said.

She put her hand on my shoulder and bent down to kiss my cheek.

"Is something troubling you?" I asked.

"Don't let my troubles upset you," she said.

"When I made the card, I thought it would make you happy. I did not mean to make you sad."

"You have never done anything to make me sad," she said. "That is why this whole thing is going to be so hard."

A cool evening breeze circled the dust around our feet.

"You should put on your blouse with the long sleeves," she said. "So you don't catch cold."

I wanted to ask her what was going to be so hard, but she pressed her finger over my lips and pointed towards the house.

She said "Go" and so I went.

One by one the men began to file out of their houses. Some carried plantains, others large Negro yams, which made your body itch if you touched them raw. There were no men in Tante Atie's and my house so we carried the food ourselves to the yard where the children had been playing.

The women entered the yard with tins of steaming ginger tea and baskets of cassava bread. Tante Atie and I sat near the gate, she behind the women and me behind the girls.

Monsieur Augustin stacked some twigs with a rusty

pitchfork and dropped his ripe plantains and husked corn on the pile. He lit a long match and dropped it on the top of the heap. The flame spread from twig to twig, until they all blended into a large smoky fire.

Monsieur Augustin's wife began to pass around large cups of ginger tea. The men broke down into small groups and strolled down the garden path, smoking their pipes. Old *tantes*—aunties—and grandmothers swayed cooing babies on their laps. The teenage boys and girls drifted to dark corners, hidden by the shadows of rustling banana leaves.

Tante Atie said that the way these potlucks started was really a long time ago in the hills. Back then, a whole village would get together and clear a field for planting. The group would take turns clearing each person's land, until all the land in the village was cleared and planted. The women would cook large amounts of food while the men worked. Then at sunset, when the work was done, everyone would gather together and enjoy a feast of eating, dancing, and laughter.

Here in Croix-des-Rosets, most of the people were city workers who labored like Tante Atie in baseball or clothing factories and lived in small cramped houses to support their families back in the provinces. Tante Atie said that we were lucky to live in a house as big as ours, with a living room to receive our guests, *plus* a room for the two of us to sleep in. Tante Atie said that only people living on New York money or people with professions, like Monsieur Augustin, could afford to live in a house where they did not have to share a yard with a pack of other people. The others had to live in huts, shacks, or one-room houses that, sometimes, they had to build themselves.

In spite of where they might live, this potluck was open to everybody who wanted to come. There was no field to plant, but the workers used their friendships in the factories or their grouping in the shared houses as a reason to get together, eat, and celebrate life.

Tante Atie kept looking at Madame Augustin as she passed the tea to each person in the women's circle around us.

"How is Martine?" Madame Augustin handed Tante Atie a cup of steaming tea. Tante Atie's hand jerked and the tea sprinkled the back of Madame Augustin's hand.

"I saw the *facteur* bring you something big yesterday." Madame Augustin blew into her tea as she spoke. "Did your sister send you a gift?"

Tante Atie tried to ignore the question.

"Was it a gift?" insisted Madame Augustin. "It is not the child's birthday again, is it? She was just twelve, no less than two months ago."

I wondered why Tante Atie had not showed me the big package. Usually, my mother would send us two cassettes with our regular money allowance. One cassette would be for me and Tante Atie, the other for my grandmother. Usually, Tante Atie and I would listen to our cassette together. Maybe she was saving it for later.

I tried to listen without looking directly at the women's faces. That would have been disrespectful, as bad as speaking without being spoken to.

"How is Martine doing over there?" asked Stéphane, the

albino's wife. She was a sequins piece worker, who made herself hats from leftover factory sequins. That night she was wearing a gold bonnet that make her look like a star had landed on her head.

"My sister is fine, thank you," Tante Atie finally answered.

Madame Augustin took a sip of her tea and looked over at me. She gave me a reprimanding look that said: Why aren't you playing with the other children? I quickly lowered my eyes, pretending to be studying some random pebbles on the ground.

"I would wager that it is very nice over there in New York," Madame Augustin said.

"I suppose it could be," said Tante Atie.

"Why have you never gone?" asked Madame Augustin.

"Perhaps it is not yet the time," said Tante Atie.

"Perhaps it is," corrected Madame Augustin.

She leaned over Tante Atie's shoulder and whispered in a not so low voice, "When are you going to tell us, Atie, when the car comes to take you to the airplane?"

"Is Martine sending for you?" asked the albino's wife.

Suddenly, all the women began to buzz with questions.

"When are you leaving?"

"Can it really be as sudden as that?"

"Will you marry there?"

"Will you remember us?"

"I am not going anywhere," Tante Atie interrupted.

"I have it on good information that it was a plane ticket that you received," said Madame Augustin. "If you are not going, then who was the plane ticket for?"

All their eyes fell on me at the same time.

"Is the mother sending for the child?" asked the albino's wife.

"I saw the delivery," said Madame Augustin. "Then she is sending for the child," they concluded. Suddenly a large hand was patting my shoulder. "This is very good news," said the accompanying voice. "It is the best thing that is ever going to happen to you."

I could not eat the bowl of food that Tante Atie laid in front of me. I only kept wishing that everyone would disappear so I could go back home.

Soon everyone began to drift towards their homes. On Saturdays there was the house to clean and water to fetch from long distances and the clothes to wash and iron for the Mother's Day Mass.

After everyone was gone, Monsieur Augustin walked Tante Atie and me home. When we got to our door he moved closer to Tante Atie as though he wanted to whisper something in her ear. She looked up at him and smiled, then quickly covered her lips with her fingers, as though she suddenly remembered her missing teeth and did not want him to see them.

He turned around to look across the street. His wife was carrying some of the pots back inside the house. He squeezed Tante Atie's hand and pressed his cheek against hers.

"It is good news, Atie," he said. "Neither you nor Sophie should be sad. A child belongs with her mother, and a mother with her child."

His wife was now sitting on the steps in front of their bougainvillea, waiting for him.

"I did not think you would tell your wife before I had a chance to tell the child," said Tante Atie to Monsieur Augustin.

"You must be brave," he said. "It is some very wonderful news for this child."

The night had grown a bit cool, but we both stood and watched as Monsieur Augustin crossed the street, took the pails from his wife's hand and bent down to kiss her forehead. He put his arms around her and closed the front door behind them.

"When you tell someone something and you call it a secret, they should know not to tell others," Tante Atie mumbled to herself.

She kept her eyes on the Augustin's house. They had electricity. The main light in their bedroom was lit. Their bodies were silhouetted on the ruffled curtains blowing in the night breeze. Monsieur Augustin sat in a rocking chair by the window. His wife sat on his lap as she unlaced her long braid of black hair. Monsieur Augustin brushed the hair draped like a silk blanket down Madame Augustin's back. When he was done, Monsieur Augustin got up to undress. Then slowly, Madame Augustin took off her day clothes and slipped into a long-sleeved nightgown. Their laughter rose in the night as they began a tickling fight. The light flickered off and they tumbled into bed.

Tante Atie kept looking at the window even after all signs of the Augustins had faded into the night.

A tear rolled down her cheek as she unbolted the door to go inside. I immediately started walking towards our bedroom. She raced after me and tried to catch up. When she did, she pressed her hand down on my shoulder and tried to turn my body around, to face her.

"Do you know why I always wished I could read?"

Her teary eyes gazed directly into mine.

"I don't know why." I tried to answer as politely as I could.

"It was always my dream to read," she said, "so I could read that old Bible under my pillow and find the answers to everything right there between those pages. What do you think that old Bible would have us do right now, about this moment?"

"I don't know," I said.

"How can you not know?" she asked. "You try to tell me there is all wisdom in reading but at a time like this you disappoint me."

"You lied!" I shouted.

She grabbed both my ears and twisted them until they burned.

I stomped my feet and walked away. As I rushed to bed, I began to take off my clothes so quickly that I almost tore them from my body.

The smell of lemon perfume stung my nose as I pulled the sheet over my head.

"I did not lie," she said, "I kept a secret, which is different. I wanted to tell you. I needed time to reconcile myself, to accept it. It was very sudden, just a cassette from Martine saying, 'I want my daughter,' and then as fast as you can put two fingers together to snap, she sends me a plane ticket with a date on it. I am not even certain that she is doing this properly. All she tells me is that she arranged it with a woman who works on the airplane."

"Was I ever going to know?" I asked.

"I was going to put you to sleep, put you in a suitcase, and send you to her. One day you would wake up there and you would feel like your whole life here with me was a dream." She tried to force a laugh, but it didn't make it past her throat. "I had this plan, you see. I thought it was a good plan. I was going to tell you this, that in one week you would be going to see your mother. As far as you would know, it would just be a visit. I felt it in my heart and took it on Monsieur Augustin's advice that, once you got there, you would love it so much that you would beg your mother to let you stay. You have heard with your own two ears what everyone has said. We have no right to be sad."

I sunk deeper and deeper into the bed and lost my body in the darkness, in the folds of the sheets.

The bed creaked loudly as Tante Atie climbed up on her side.

"Don't you ever tell anyone that I cry when I watch Donald and his wife getting ready for bed," she said, sobbing.

I groped for my clothes in the dark and found the Mother's Day card I had made her. I tucked it under her pillow as I listened to her mumble some final words in her sleep.

2

· ❧ ❧ ❧ ·

The smell of cinnamon rice pudding scented the whole kitchen. Tante Atie was sitting at the table with a bowl in front of her when I came in. I felt closer to tears with each word I even thought of saying, so I said nothing.

I sat at my usual place at the table and watched out of the corner of my eyes as she poured a bowl of rice pudding and slid it towards me. Breakfast rice pudding was a special treat.

"Bonjou," she said, waving a spoon in front of my face. "Your *bonjou*, your greeting, is your passport."

I kept my head down and took the spoon only when she laid it down in front of me. I did not feel like eating, but if I did not eat, we would have had to sit and stare at one another, and sooner or later, one of us would have had to say something.

I picked up the spoon and began to eat. Tante Atie's lips spread into a little grin as she watched me. Her laughter prefaced the start of what was going to be a funny story. There were many stories that Tante Atie liked to tell. There were mostly sad stories, but every once in a while, there was a funny one. There was the time when she was a little girl, when my grandmother was a practicing Protestant. Granmè Ifé tried to show her Christian faith by standing over the edge of a snake pit and ordering the devils back into the ground. Tante Atie was always bent over with laughter as she remembered the look on Granmè Ifé's face when one of the snakes started to crawl up the side of the pit towards her. My grandmother did not come out for days after that.

Whether something was funny or not depended on the way Tante Atie told it. That morning, she could not bring the laughter out of me like she had in the past. It was even hard for her to force it out of herself.

After I had eaten, I washed the dishes and put them in the basket to dry.

"I want to tell you a few things," Tante Atie said from where she was sitting at the table. "You need to know certain things about your mother."

"Why can't you come to New York too?" I interrupted.

"Because it is not the time yet. After you leave, I am going back home to take care of your grandmother. I am only here in Croix-des-Rosets because of your schooling. Once you leave, I can go back."

"I don't know why you can't go to New York too," I said.

"We are each going to our mothers. That is what was supposed to happen. Your mother wants to see you now, Sophie. She does not want you to forget who your *real* mother is. When she left you with me, she and I, we agreed that it would only be for a while. You were just a baby then. She left you because she was going to a place she knew nothing about. She did not want to take chances with you."

Tante Atie opened the front door and let the morning sun inside. She ran her fingers along the grilled iron as she looked up at the clear indigo sky.

She picked up a broom and began to sweep the mosaic floor.

"My angel," she said, "I would like to know that by word or by example I have taught you love. I must tell you that I do love your mother. Everything I love about you, I loved in her first. That is why I could never fight her about keeping you here. I do not want you to go and fight with her either. In this country, there are many good reasons for mothers to abandon their children." She stopped to pound the dust out of the living room cushions. "But you were never abandoned. You were with me. Your mother and I, when we were children we had no control over anything. Not even this body." She pounded her fist over her chest and stomach. "When my father died, my mother had to dig a hole and just drop him in it. We are a family with dirt under our fingernails. Do you know what that means?"

She did not wait for me to answer.

"That means we've worked the land. We're not *educated*. My father would have never dreamt that we would live in the same kind of house that people like Monsieur and Madame Augustin live in. He, a schoolteacher, and we, daughters of the hills, old peasant stock, *pitit sòyèt*, ragamuffins. If we can live here, if you have this door open to you, it is because of your mother. Promise me that you are not going to fight with your mother when you get there."

"I am not going to fight," I said.

"Good," she said. "It would be a shame if the two of you got into battles because you share a lot more than you know."

She reached over and touched the collar of my lemon-toned housedress.

"Everything you own is yellow," she said, "wildflower yellow, like dandelions, sunflowers."

"And daffodils," I added.

"That is right," she said, "your mother, she loved daffodils."

Tante Atie told me that my mother loved daffodils because they grew in a place that they were not supposed to. They were really European flowers, French buds and stems, meant for colder climates. A long time ago, a French woman had brought them to Croix-des-Rosets and planted them there. A strain of daffodils had grown that could withstand the heat, but they were the color of pumpkins and golden summer squash, as though they had acquired a bronze tinge from the skin of the natives who had adopted them.

Tante Atie took the card from her pocket and put it on the night table, next to the plane ticket. She said that it would be nice for me to give the card to my mother personally, even though the daffodil was gone.

3

· ❀ ❀ ❀ ·

The trip to La Nouvelle Dame Marie took a few hours in a rocky van. However, Tante Atie thought that I couldn't leave for New York without my grandmother's blessing. Besides, Granmè Ifé was getting on in years and this could be my last chance to see her.

The van from Croix-des-Rosets let us off in the marketplace in La Nouvelle Dame Marie. The roads to my grandmother's house were too rough for anything but wheelbarrows, mules, or feet.

Tante Atie and I decided to go on foot. We walked by a line of thatched huts where a group of women were pounding millet in a large mortar with a pestle. Others were roasting large cassava cakes in flat pans over charcoal pits.

In the cane fields, the men chopped cane stalks as they sang back and forth to one another. A crammed wheelbarrow rolled towards us. We stepped aside and allowed the boys to pass. They were bare-chested and soaked with sweat, with no protection from the sun except old straw hats.

We passed a farm with a bamboo fence around it. The owner was Man Grace, a tall woman who had hair patches growing out of her chin. Man Grace and her daughter were working in the yard, throwing handfuls of purple corn at a flock of guinea fowls.

My mother had sent money for the reconstruction of her old home. The house stood out from all the others in La Nouvelle Dame Marie. It was a flat red brick house with wide windows and a shingled roof. A barbed wire fence bordered my grandmother's pumpkin vines and tuberose stems.

I raced up to the front of the house to stand under the rooster-shaped weather vanes spinning on my grandmother's porch. My grandmother was in the yard, pulling a rope out of her stone well.

"Old woman, I brought your child," Tante Atie said.

The rope slipped out of my grandmother's hands, the bucket crashing with an echoing splash. I leaped into her arms, nearly knocking her down.

"It does my heart a lot of good to see you," she said.

Tante Atie kissed my grandmother on the cheek and then went inside the house.

Granmè Ifé wrapped her arms around my body. Her head came up to my chin, her mop of shrubby white hair tickling my lips.

"Are you hungry?" she asked. "I am going to cook only the things you like."

We ate supper on the back porch. My grandmother cooked rice and Congo beans with sun-dried mushrooms. She was wearing a long black dress, as part of her *dèy*, to mourn my grandfather.

"Tell me, what good things have you been doing?" asked my grandmother.

"She has been getting all the highest marks in school," said Tante Atie. "Her mother will be very proud."

"You must never forget this," said my grandmother. "Your mother is your first friend."

I slept alone in the third room in the house. It had a large four-poster bed and a mahogany wardrobe with giant hibiscus carved all over it. The mattress sank as I slipped under the sheets in the bed. It was nice to have a bed of my own every so often.

I lay in bed, waiting for the nightmare where my mother would finally get to take me away.

We left the next day to return to Croix-des-Rosets. Tante Atie had to go back to work. Besides, my grandmother said that it was best that we leave before she got too used to us and suffered a sudden attack of chagrin.

To my grandmother, chagrin was a genuine physical disease. Like a hurt leg or a broken arm. To treat chagrin, you drank tea from leaves that only my grandmother and other old wise women could recognize.

We each gave my grandmother two kisses as she urged us to go before she kept us for good.

"Can one really die of chagrin?" I asked Tante Atie in the van on the way back.

She said it was not a sudden illness, but something that

could kill you slowly, taking a small piece of you every day until one day it finally takes all of you away.

"How can we keep it from happening to us?" I asked.

"We don't choose it," she said, "it chooses us. A horse has four legs, but it can fall anyway."

She told me about a group of people in Ginen who carry the sky on their heads. They are the people of Creation. Strong, tall, and mighty people who can bear anything. Their Maker, she said, gives them the sky to carry because they are strong. These people do not know who they are, but if you see a lot of trouble in your life, it is because you were chosen to carry part of the sky on your head.